THE BRIDESMAID AND THE HURRICANE

A CAPITAL KISSES NOVEL

KELLY MAHER

D INK EDITIONS

Published by D Ink Editions, July 2017.

Trade paper ISBN-13: 978-0996847759

EBook ISBN-13: 978-0996847742

Production contractors:

Cover designer: Romanced by the Cover

Editor: Latoya C. Smith, LCS Literary Services

Copyeditor: Lynda Ryba, FWS Media

Proofreader: Lillie Applegarth, Lillie's Literary Services

Any remaining errors are to be blamed on the author.

As this is a work of fiction, any resemblance to a real person, event, or policy is completely coincidental.

Copyright © 2017 by Kelly Maher

All rights reserved.

No part of this book may be reproduced in any form or by any electronic or mechanical means, including information storage and retrieval systems, without written permission from the author, except for the use of brief quotations in a book review.

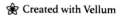 Created with Vellum

ALSO BY KELLY MAHER

PRINT

BEST EROTIC ROMANCE 2014, edited by Kristina Wright
includes Kelly's story "Closing the Deal"
DUTY AND DESIRE, edited by Kristina Wright
includes Kelly's story "Homecoming"
LUST AT FIRST BITE, edited by Lindsay Gordon
includes Kelly's story "Feasting"
THE SEXY LIBRARIAN'S BIG BOOK OF EROTICA,
edited by Rose Caraway
includes Kelly's story "Notes on a Scandal"

EBOOK

Capital Kisses series
BLIZZARD BLISS (prequel short story)

Sweet Heat series (previously published stories)
SWEET HEAT, VOLUME 1
SWEET HEAT, VOLUME 2
SWEET HEAT, VOLUME 3

A one-weekend stand over a year ago, and now they're coworkers...

Being a woman in TV is hard enough, but when her boss is trying to derail Radhika O'Leary's career from behind the scenes, she has to make sure every aspect of her work—and her life—stands up to scrutiny.

Of course, the double standard is alive and well and Malcolm Jones, the broadcast meteorologist known as "Colm" to his friends and "The Hurricane Hottie" to his fangirls, knows that fame can hurt just as much as it helps. When Colm moves to DC, he's excited to work with Radhika—her professional reputation is sparkling, and so are the kisses they shared that one weekend over a year ago when he was in town covering a blizzard.

But when Radhika is paired up with Colm for a project, all she sees is a looming storm over her carefully constructed career. Sparks still fly between the two journalists, and if they're not careful, lightning might strike and alter the course of their lives forever.

~

Find out more about the Capital Kisses world by signing up for Kelly's newsletter at www.kellymaher.com/contact.

This book is dedicated to my Grandma B. who passed away at the age of 99 the day before I began drafting it. Grandma, you weren't a romance reader, and we didn't always see eye-to-eye on things, but I know you were proud of the work I did and wanted the best for me. I miss you.

1

"Thanks for calling me. I enjoyed meeting with you, and maybe we can discuss other opportunities in the future." As Radhika O'Leary surveyed the buildings surrounding the office complex's small courtyard, the woman at the other end of the line hummed and Radhika knew she wouldn't be hearing about future opportunities at that station. Goddamned Bella. You'd think with how much grief her boss gave her, she'd want Radhika gone as much as Radhika wanted to be gone.

She hung up and rolled her neck, trying to work out some of the tension gathered in her shoulders. No way could she go to the meeting welcoming the network's newest star, Malcolm Jones, not that she'd been planning on going anyway. No need to cross paths with Colm again if she could help it. And strangling her boss, Bella DiNunzio, in front of the entire station would make a *great* reunion impression.

Drawing in a deep breath, she savored what smell of green and sea she could pick up amongst the car exhaust. Maybe she could talk her girlfriends into a day trip out to the Eastern Shore, or even down to Virginia Beach. She headed back into the office, waving at the guards. After getting off the elevator, she was about to turn the corner toward her portion of the cubicle farm when she nearly ran into her favorite video editor.

Lisa jumped back. "Hey, Radhika."

"Hey, Lisa. Is Bella skulking around?"

"Not that I saw. I'm grabbing a cup of coffee before the meet and greet. Want to come with me?"

"No. I've got some things I need to take care of. Bella to avoid."

"You're skipping the Hurricane Hottie?"

Radhika managed to stop herself from rolling her eyes. Why on Earth had they anointed Colm with that stupid nickname?

"No. I'm not going to meet Mr. Jones." Especially as she'd more than met him already. Nerves in her stomach battled with a blooming heat a little farther south as she remembered those two nights.

Lisa nudged her and waggled her brows. "You sure you don't want to meet the station's newest celebrity?"

"I'm sure. You go have fun."

Lisa shook her head. "I don't know what to do with you. You haven't dated anyone since Vince."

"And I'm planning on keeping it that way. I'm better off alone." Discreet hook-ups were fine, if she could be bothered to find the time to screen remotely reasonable candidates. Colm was decidedly an aberration and would stay that way. Stupid hormones.

"You say that now, but wait until your brother moves out and you have that fabulous condo all to yourself."

"Rory's not going anywhere for a while. Cecilia's got him thinking of going back to school, and if he does that, he's going to need money for tuition rather than rent."

"Good luck to him. I've got to get going if I'm going to get my coffee."

"Have fun."

Lisa waved and headed for the elevator. On her way to her cube, Radhika pulled out her phone and pulled up her company email. Just a reminder about how everyone should be hands on deck to greet Colm. A text popped up from her fellow producer Ed a minute later.

> E: *You going to the meet and greet?*
>
> R: *No.*
>
> E: *Shit, girl. You're missing the Hurricane Hottie?*
>
> R: *Not you, too?*
>
> E: *Married, not dead. Besides, Harold wants his autograph. I get good husband points if I get it for him.*

Radhika snorted and told him good luck. She had a feeling at this point the meet and greet would be packed, with barely any room to move around.

She sat down and worked for a bit. Her area was dead other than the few people she could hear scrambling for updates on stories being featured on the local midday newscast. She checked her watch. Everyone should be gathered at the meeting now. The perfect time to get lunch for the day from one of the food trucks. She headed to the elevators, keeping an eye out in case Bella popped out of the ether like the devil she was. Thankfully, no stragglers were waiting, which also meant she had no one to bitch to as the elevators took forever to come.

The elevator doors opened to reveal none other than the Hurricane Hottie himself standing inside. She was sure the laughter she heard echoing in her head belonged to some goddess of fate.

He was doing something on his phone, so he didn't immediately spot her. She had time to study how his golden hair seemed to have lightened a shade or two. His skin had warmed in tone from the fair paleness of her memories, so she assumed the cause of both was the southern sun from his last posting. Not that she'd been tracking his moves since the previous January. At least, not obsessively. The doors started to close again and she scooted in. She kept her head down, in the hopes he wouldn't see her, and wished she'd taken her hair out of its ponytail so it could screen her face from view.

She was reaching for the buttons in front of him when his deep voice slid over her, reminding her of silken sheets. Well, they'd been hotel cotton, but to her body, with him, they'd felt like the finest silk. "What floor?"

"Uh, lobby. Please."

His head snapped up and he stared at her. "Radhika?"

She swallowed. "Yes."

His lips spread into a smile and then a full-on grin. He hit the emergency stop button and lifted his arms, but stopped with inches to spare. "Uh, can I hug you?"

Surprised that he not only remembered her face and her name after nearly eighteen months, but that he wanted to touch her again, her body screamed yes, but her brain tried to bat the impulse down. She started to respond, but her throat closed. She cleared it. "Sure. Sure."

His arms were just as strong and his back as tough with muscle as she remembered and heat filled her body. He didn't do anything but hug her. Kind of like when Rory hugged her. Oh, God. A former lover was hugging her just as her brother did. Could this get any more embarrassing?

"Hey, Radhika? You need help in there?"

Yep. There it was.

When Colm stepped back with his hands up, looking around for the camera, she reached over and pressed the intercom button. "Hey, Denise. I'm good. We'll get moving again in a sec."

"You let me know if you want me to send a team up, girl. I don't care who he is."

"Appreciate it, Denise."

Colm had finally spotted the camera and waved at it. "Sorry for the inconvenience, Denise."

A sniff was clearly heard before the connection cut out. Radhika pressed the emergency stop button to get the car moving again. "You do not want to get on Denise's bad side."

He nodded. "I got that impression when I signed in this morning. Are you coming to the shindig?"

"Uh, no. I've got some things to do and need to get lunch now before I get nothing."

Was it her imagination, or did his shoulders slump the

tiniest bit? "Okay. I'm sorry you won't be there. Would you like to go out for drinks later?"

She froze, not believing what she was hearing. Drinks? Her eyes narrowed and she studied him. He appeared relaxed with his hands in his pockets, and his arms loose. Temptation nibbled at her, but working for Bella was bad enough already. She needed to avoid any appearance of salacious fraternizing. Her boss had been gleeful when she'd had one of Radhika's former coworkers written up for violating company policy. "Sorry. I'm meeting a friend for dinner."

"A boyfriend?"

Yep. His shoulders had definitely tensed. The tiniest bit, but she'd spent enough time with that body. Even if it had been over a year ago. "No. A girlfriend."

"Oh. Ohhhhhh. Okay."

"Not that kind of girlfriend, either."

Another smile bloomed on his lips. "So, you're single?"

Of course, the elevator doors would open right as he asked that and a clutch of the biggest gossips in the office were standing there waiting to get on. She could at least trust Denise to keep her mouth shut. But these women and men? She spotted someone's thumbs flying across the face of her phone already. No way in hell was she going to the meeting now. Radhika pursed her lips and moved to the opposite corner from him as the others filed into the elevator. The chatter as they fawned over Colm grated on Radhika's nerves, but they were soon at the floor where the meeting rooms were. As Colm was pulled out of the elevator by his fan group, he looked over his shoulder and mouthed the word "Later" at her. She kept her eyes on his and shook her head as the doors closed. When they finally cut him off from view, she slumped against the wall. She was so fucked.

Radhika stopped by the security desk on her way out and asked to see Denise. The guard radioed the request and Denise radioed back telling him to send her back to the monitor room. Radhika thanked the desk guard and headed back. She knocked on the door.

"Come on in."

Radhika smiled at her friend as she walked in. "Thanks for checking on me."

"I wanted to make sure you were good. You had this panicked look on your face."

Radhika sat down in one of the chairs off to the side. "Yeah, well, I wasn't expecting to see him. I thought everyone was already in the meeting room."

Denise kept her gaze on the security monitors. She zoomed in briefly on one of the outside cameras, and then held her finger up. She called the guards outside. Within a minute, they came into view and were shuffling off a guy who'd decided to take a piss on the building in the middle of the morning. Radhika held up a hand to block her view so she didn't have to watch him stuffing his dick back into his pants.

"So. You and the Hurricane Hottie?"

Radhika waved her hand. "It's nothing. We met last year when he was in town covering the blizzard."

Denise raised a brow. "Um-hmmm. I know what can go on in those hotels. I've had to break up a few fights between people married to other people as they're walking in the door."

"Yeah, that's not going to happen here. I do not date or sleep with coworkers. Not happening." Not anymore. Fresh resolve filled her. She'd been burned enough in that regard.

Denise shrugged. "You're single, and so is he. What you do on your own time is your business. Don't bring it into the office making me or anyone else deal with it and we're good."

Radhika laughed. "I'm surprised anyone tries to cross you, Denise."

"They don't try more than once. Now, are you down here to talk to me or do something else?"

"I was going to grab lunch from one of the trucks."

"Good." She reached into the back pocket of her pants and pulled out a bill. "If the taco truck is here, can you get me an order of the Korean beef with sriracha sauce?"

"Will do."

"Thanks."

Outside, she surveyed her choices and decided to go with the tacos herself. If the arepa truck had been here today, she would have had a much harder decision. She got two orders of what Denise requested and headed back to the office. She stopped at the monitor room to deliver Denise her food and change, then headed up to her own floor.

It was mostly deserted, which meant the meet and greet was still going.

"Radhika."

She closed her eyes, cursing the gods of fate that seemed to have it out for her today. Radhika turned around with a tight smile. Her boss stood there in an immaculately pressed pantsuit, her dark brown hair pulled back in a soft twist. "Yes?"

"Did you finish the timing of that tape for Ed?"

"Yes, he's got it and will be working on it as soon as he's out of the meeting."

Bella grunted. "Why aren't you there?"

Trying not to grit her teeth, she clenched the fingers of her free hand behind her back. "I wanted to get a head start on the story about the college students who lost their scholarships."

"Good. Your time's been cut by thirty seconds."

"What?"

"Not my fault. Do it."

Radhika closed her eyes, but nodded even though Bella had already turned and headed to her office.

It may not be Bella's fault that the request was made, but she didn't need to approve all the requests to cut time out of Radhika's assignments. At least this was one of the up-and-coming on-air talent's stories, so Radhika could sic him on Bella. She'd learned within the first days of working for her that in Bella's eyes, the producers below her were nothing but barely-tolerated lackeys. If anything needed doing, it was the on-air talent who could get around her. She should have listened to her gut when she got this job, but panic over the fallout from Vince had blinded her. One more thing to blame on him. Radhika sat down in her chair and sent an email to the reporter to let him know and then began reviewing the story notes to see where it could be cut in case he couldn't get around Bella.

Once she was done with that, she dug into her tacos.

She was on the last taco when the filling had the audacity to fall out the back and down the front of her shirt. "God-fucking-dammit."

"Tsk-tsk. And this being such a professional organization."

Radhika closed her eyes. First she ran into him unprepared in the elevator. Then got caught by her favorite security guard hugging him. Then he had the nerve to ask her if she was single, while standing near the biggest gossips in the office. Now, he had to be the one hearing her swear over a ruined shirt. She was stopping at the liquor store on the way home and buying the biggest bottle of vodka they had.

"Hi, Colm. How was the meeting?"

He came over and leaned his gorgeously fit ass on her desk. Wool slacks should not look that sexy. She bit back a sigh. He took one look at the taco filling now sitting in her lap, then handed her one of the napkins lying next to his thick thigh. "Pretty good. I got a little tired of signing autographs, though."

Knowing some of her coworkers, she winced. "No one asked you to sign a body part, did they?"

"Nope. That, thankfully, has been reserved by use of fans at promotional events."

"Seriously?"

"A few even said they were heading straight to the tattoo parlor to have it immortalized. I think my signature is sitting next to Bruce Springsteen's on some woman's breast."

Unsure how to respond, she kept her head down as she mopped up the filling and sauce. The dry-cleaning bill for both the shirt and the pants was going to be a bitch. She should just toss them. In fact, she should probably take some personal leave and go buy a whole new outfit. It's not like she could go to the planning meeting she had this afternoon in the remnants of bulgogi and sriracha sauce. Especially with Bella being there.

"So, drinks?"

"I never agreed to drinks."

"Yeah, we got a little distracted there. What about tomorrow night?"

This time, Radhika met his gaze. The way he was smiling made her think of an overgrown leprechaun. "Are you always this pushy?"

He held up his hands and scooched back on the desk. "You can say no. It's cool."

She let out a breath she hadn't quite realized she'd been holding. "I appreciate that. I'm going to say no to drinks. I don't date coworkers."

His brows rose and he leaned in closer. Thank you, sweet baby Jesus, he kept the volume of his voice down. "What about the blizzard?"

"We weren't coworkers then. Plus, you were my rebound." Why she thought her rebound should be another fabulous-looking news guy after Vince, she had no clue. It had to have been the pheromone fumes. Even now, she had to beat back the impulse to bury her nose in his neck and smell him.

His brows rose. "Fair enough. Would you say we're platonic friends?"

"As I am with all of my coworkers." She sipped from the bottle of water she kept at her desk.

"Perfect. Then I need you as my pretend date."

She spewed the mouthful she'd taken and gave even more thanks that it was only water and not pop as she sprayed his fancy suit. He grabbed another napkin and began dabbing at the moisture.

"Excuse me?"

"My pretend date. My sister is throwing a party for me on Saturday to welcome me to DC and she ordered me to bring a date."

"Why would your sister order you to bring a date?"

"Apparently to protect me from the pack of hungry lions she calls friends."

"Then why is she friends with them?"

He shrugged shoulders broader than anyone should be blessed with. "I'm assuming it's a woman thing. You can be friends with me, but you can't date my baby brother."

Radhika narrowed her eyes at him. "How far apart in age are you?"

"A year."

"Yeah, that explains it."

"What?"

"I've got a younger brother, too, but he's seven years younger than me. I'd kick the ass of any girl who dared to break his heart, but none of my friends ever had their eyes on him in that way when we were growing up. You guys are close enough in age that you were date-worthy material for her friends in school."

Colm scanned the cube farm, a thoughtful expression on his face. When he continued sitting like that for more than a minute, she tapped his thigh with her pointer finger. Goddamn, the muscle there. She could not think about sinking her teeth into it. His hungry lions comparison was way too apt.

He glanced down at her, and his eyes cleared. "That explains a lot. Thanks."

"Whatever. I've got work to do."

"You haven't said yet if you'd be my pretend date."

"No."

"But, you're the only single person I know here whom I trust not to maul me. Come over. It starts at four."

"I can't. I've got plans with friends."

"What?"

"Bridal party shopping. I have no idea how long it will take." She knew for sure it would be over by four so one of her best friends, Stacey, could head to the theater for show prep.

"Come after. My sister wouldn't have insisted if she didn't think it was important. You'd be doing me a huge favor. Plus, you can give me the inside dirt on everyone here outside of work."

Radhika rocked back in her chair. "You're persistent."

"Had to be to get where I'm at. The house is up in Brookland, so I can come pick you up...where do you live, by the way?"

"I can get to Brookland just fine on my own." As soon as the words rolled out of her mouth, she knew they were the wrong ones to say.

He grinned. If he'd been at all boyish looking, she would have compared him to an eager puppy. "So, you'll go?"

Dammit. She felt boxed in. She'd been thinking about calling Jorie, another of her best friends, to see if she wanted to go out for dinner after they finished bridesmaid duties, because her brother Rory had asked for some private time with Cecilia. She could lie, but there was something about him that made everything rebel at uttering the tiniest untruth to him. She sighed. "Sure. Send me the address and I'll meet you there." She rattled off her work email. He pulled out his phone and tapped it in.

"Got it. What's your cell number?"

"Why?"

"In case you get lost or something comes up. I'll text you so you have mine."

Damn logic. She gave him her number, and within moments, the chime notifying her of a text rang on her phone.

Someone tapped on the wall of her cubicle and she looked over her shoulder to see the reporter from the scholarship story standing there.

"Hey, Lee. Have you met Colm Jones, yet?"

"Yeah, man. Congrats on that photo spread."

It was only because she'd been watching his face that she caught the twitch of muscle in Colm's cheek. "Thanks. Nice to meet you. I'll catch you later, Radhika."

"Later."

Lee managed to wait until Colm had left. "I hear you're seeing him. Is that smart?"

She should have put a timer on the gossip circuit. "I'm not seeing him, Lee."

"That's not what Yvonne said."

She stared at him for a full minute before he began squirming. "Yvonne is one of the biggest gossips in the office, and you know that. Remember that thing in journalism school about vetting your sources?"

"She usually has superior intel. Something had to have happened if she was saying that."

"Nothing. Nothing happened."

"Remember that other saying about protesting too much?"

"Screw that. How are you going to deal with Bella?"

Radhika hashed out a plan of attack with Lee and left it in his hands to execute. She checked her email after he left and found an intra-office newsletter recapping the welcome party for Colm. Rubbing her chest, she read through it. The party was standard, and the photos would be good for publicity.

She shouldn't have agreed to meet him outside of work. Her heart knew the pain of mixing business with pleasure and her heart always lost.

2

A couple days later, Radhika was clipping the scholarship story to include the fifteen seconds Lee had been able to weasel out of Bella when she heard her name shouted from the hallway. Good God. Didn't any of her friends have any sense? She sent the notes off to Lee for approval before locking her computer and getting up. Stacey was talking with one of her coworkers. When she caught sight of Radhika, she squealed, ran over, and hugged her. Actresses. The ultimate drama queens.

"Chill out, Stace."

Stacey brushed her soft brown curls behind her ear. The makeup she'd worn for her TV appearance highlighted her hazel eyes, made even brighter by her grin. With the sprinkling of freckles on her cheeks, dulled only a bit by the makeup, she looked like an ad for Ireland. "Oh, you know how I get when I'm on TV. Plus, I know this embarrasses the hell out you. Besides, they keep asking me to come on the show, so I haven't pissed off anyone truly important."

Radhika leaned back. "Why are you my friend again?"

"You felt bad about puking on us."

Radhika's coworker headed off, waving goodbye. "I shouldn't have asked."

"Probably not. Where can we grab some lunch?"

"Food trucks or cafeteria?"

Stacey scrunched her nose. "Cafeteria. I didn't check to see which trucks are out there and I need to watch what I'm eating right now."

Radhika whipped her head around as she pressed the button for the elevator. "What? Why?"

"It's nothing. I've started getting a sore stomach, so my doctor wants me eating bland foods for a bit. Nothing to worry about."

"How bad is the stomach?"

"Bad enough that I went to my doctor about it. I'm hoping it's just nerves over the opening of the show and that it'll be over once we get through opening weekend."

"Fingers crossed."

Once they got inside the cafeteria, they went their separate ways to order their lunches. Stacey came back as Radhika was waiting on the veggie burger she'd ordered. "Did you get fries to go with that?"

"Yes."

"Can you get a second order? I've been dying for some."

"Sure." She put in the request and they came up with the burger.

They went through the check out and Radhika put it all on her company account. They found an empty table over in one of the corners. Less chance of being interrupted. "How did the segment go?"

"Really good. I managed to get in all of the information I wanted to about the show and we still had a little time left over, so I talked a bit about how part of the proceeds go to help charity."

"That's great."

"Yeah. Hopefully, if someone doesn't go to the play, they'll still consider donating." She lifted one shoulder and dug into her bowl of chicken noodle soup.

The noise level in the cafeteria lifted like a small wave building into a bigger one. Radhika looked over and quickly found the reason. Colm. She wondered if this was his first turn in the cafeteria. Like if he knew that tour groups sometimes ended up here. Today, there was a bunch of high schoolers and some family groups. High-pitched squeals echoed every few seconds as he stopped to take pictures she was sure would be posted to the internet right after he walked away.

"Wow. Is that him?"

Radhika turned back to find Stacey staring at Colm slack jawed. "Mm-hmmm."

Stacey leaned in. "And you hit that?" She held up her hand for a high-five.

Radhika let her hang.

"Hey, I'm trying to congratulate you."

"You realize that's crass."

"So?" She pointed at her still raised hand with her other index finger. "High-five back, bitch."

Not wanting to instigate a scene, which wouldn't take much with Stacey, Radhika high-fived her back. "I should never have told you about him. Are we done now?"

"No. I want to meet him. Who's that with him?"

Radhika looked at Colm and saw Bella standing behind him. What the hell? "My boss. I am so not going over there."

"That's the skanky-ass bitch from hell?"

"Keep your voice down."

"I am. Want me to hiss? I promise you that carries a lot more than a low murmur."

"Stacey."

"I'm just saying. Oh, look, here they come."

Radhika blinked, afraid to look away from Stacey's face in case she was correct. She could handle Colm, no problem, but Bella as well?

"Hey, Radhika. I'm glad I caught you."

Radhika turned with a smile on her face. It was the polite thing to do. "Hi, Colm. Bella."

Her boss didn't even bother to acknowledge her. The woman's eyes were plastered on Colm's ass. Jesus. Her boss was panting after him, too? Did everyone want him?

"I wanted to let you know some of the plans changed."

Stacey looked at her, and tapped her chin with her fingers. "Plans, Radhika?"

Ignoring Stacey, she nodded her head. "No problem. Why don't you email them to me?"

Colm grinned. "Great. I'll see you at three, then."

"Three? You two have a meeting today?" Of course, that's when Bella would drag her attention away from his ass.

Thankfully, she still wasn't paying any attention to Radhika, so she minutely shook her head and hoped that Colm got the clue not to let Bella know anything about meeting outside the office.

"Uh, no. Tomorrow, actually."

"Oh, good. I would hate to cut our private meeting short." The woman actually purred. *Purred.* Not surprising as she had a reputation for being a cougar, but still. Couldn't her behavior be construed as sexual harassment? Cold-cocking her boss wouldn't be the wisest move even with their history before Colm's arrival. Of course, she could pass it off on that rather than the flare of ridiculous jealousy coursing through her. She reminded herself of her promise to avoid unnecessary interactions with Bella, let alone instigating anything.

Radhika caught the tightening of Colm's jaw. It was on the tip of her tongue to offer to let them sit at the table, but before she could say anything, Stacey butted in.

"Colm, nice to meet you. I'm Stacey, one of Radhika's best friends. We were just saying the other day at brunch that she needs a date to our friends' wedding and you'd be perfect. How's your schedule looking for August?" She capped it by holding her hand out for him to shake.

Even Bella looked, for once, stunned into silence. Until she wasn't. "Who are you?"

"Stacey Hardwicke. One of Radhika's best friends. Weren't you listening?"

Radhika winced. She'd hear about this later.

Bella's wine-painted lips pulled down at the corners. "Members of the public generally aren't allowed in the cafeteria unless they're on a tour."

Stacey smiled back. "Well, bless your heart. It helps that I was one of the guests on the midday news broadcast now, doesn't it? Your anchors are the sweetest. I just love visiting with them."

Oh, Christ. When Stacey's southern accent started coming out thick as honey along with the "bless your hearts," blood was about to be spilled. Radhika grabbed her phone out of her back pocket of her trousers and turned it on. "Well, look at the time. Stacey, didn't you say you had a meeting with your agent this afternoon before the preview? I shouldn't be keeping you like this."

Stacey's smile at Bella was all teeth. Perfectly matched, whiter than toothpaste, and the envy of at least two state beauty pageant queens. According to Stace. "So nice to meet you. Colm, we'll have to talk more sometime when I'm here next."

Radhika was afraid to look up, knowing that Bella was probably staring daggers at her, but she heard the amusement in Colm's voice. "I'd love to, Stacey. Come on, Bella. Let's get this meeting over with."

Stacey watched them as they walked across the room. "That man does have brains. He'd be good for you."

"Stop trying to match make. And start a fight."

"But she is soooooo asking for one. Bitch has no power over me."

"She does over me."

Stacey had the courtesy to hunch her shoulders at that. "Oh, damn. I'm sorry, Radhika."

"Don't worry. If it's not one thing with her, it's another. I can't believe she was that blatant about Colm, though."

"That lady does not care. Is she someone's sister?"

Radhika took a bite of her burger before answering. "I have no clue. The rumor mill said she was sleeping with someone up top when she first started, but if she's chasing after other guys, that can't be too smart."

"Why did you come work here again?"

"Because they offered me a job and I thought I could learn

something from her. She'd always been professional when I ran into her at industry events."

"Working with someone is entirely different than working for someone."

"True. I've heard some people had issues with her, but as far as I know, none of them had it this bad."

Stacey reached out and squeezed her hand. "I know something's going to come through soon for you. I've got a feeling."

Radhika shook her head. "You and your feelings. Eat some of your fries before they get cold."

"Awww. You're so good to me."

"Drama queen."

"He really would be a fabulous date for the wedding."

Radhika slumped in her chair and covered her face with her hands.

Colm had been in a lot of meetings since coming on board a few days ago. He'd been looking forward to the challenge of a new job in a new city, even if it was a city he'd visited numerous times. The distraction was exactly what he needed after this last year.

At first he'd done what any healthy guy would do when being named one of the most eligible bachelors by a national publication and had taken advantage of the party invitations and offers of dates. It had gotten old quickly once he realized most of the women seriously pursuing him were doing so for what they could get out of him. Especially his last girlfriend. He'd been way too slow figuring out she was an experienced con artist.

His lawyer was still extracting him from loans she'd taken out using his name.

And, yet, Bella DiNunzio left them all in the shade. He was trying hard not to get too creeped out by her. Sure, they weren't in the same organizational command line, so she couldn't do anything to him, but he had never been so obviously hit on by someone he worked with, even after he'd given out very clear "we are only coworkers" signals. More, he wanted to steal Radhika from her.

He'd been studying Radhika's work, and after talking with reporters she'd been assigned to, he knew she would be perfect for the project he was heading. She apparently had no trouble ignoring the two hot nights they spent together. It stung, maybe more than a little, but if she could, he could. He hoped she would consider not ignoring him for at least a little while.

Then Bella's leg touched his. He moved his legs away, but hers followed. He looked her straight in the eye. "Bella, I don't like being touched."

She smiled in a way he was sure she thought was sexy, but honestly, a hungry wolf's smile was nicer. "I'm sure I can find a way to touch you that you'll like."

Goddamn it all to hell. While he was open to the possibility of some fun times without strings attached, it wasn't going to be with this woman. He stood up even though he was leaving half his lunch on the table. "Bella, this is inappropriate. I'll email you later about my proposal."

He walked out of the cafeteria and saw Radhika and her friend standing at the elevators. Grinning, he took his time in studying her back. Slim, with her dark hair hitting at her shoulders, he couldn't help but admire the way her pants cupped her butt. Heat flashed through him as he remembered when there'd been no fabric between his hand and that butt.

She was leaning in and talking heatedly with her friend. Stacey was a bit on the quirky side, but it was a fun quirky, not a cup your balls and run away in fear kind of quirky. He walked up behind them, Stacey facing him and Radhika with her back to him. Stacey didn't even blink an eyelid though he knew damn well she'd seen him walking up.

"I don't understand why you won't ask him. It's not like you two haven't done the down and dirty together. Multiple times."

He raised his brows at that little revelation. Had Radhika been talking about their nights together? Maybe they could pick things up again. Though, if she was on the project? That would be crossing the line he just ran from. He'd have to figure out a way to move that line so it wouldn't be an issue.

"Would you keep your voice down? I really should never have told you guys about that."

"Well, you did and that cat is not only out of the bag, it's on its way to Jersey."

Radhika's shoulders tensed and he saw her raise her hand to her brow. Stacey really shouldn't be torturing her like this, but it was so much fun to watch. He leaned against the wall so that Radhika could see him out of the corner of her eye. "So, when's the wedding? I want to make sure it's on my calendar."

Radhika squeaked and jumped a foot. He wondered if she was on the office basketball team with that kind of vertical jump. "Where did you come from?"

"The cafeteria. Same as you."

"You were eating with Bella."

"For all of five minutes, and then I wasn't."

"Why?"

Not wanting to talk shit about her boss to her, he lifted a shoulder. "I ended up not liking what I ordered, so I decided to make a run down to one of the food trucks. Which one would you recommend?"

Radhika stared at him, her eyes moving. She probably was trying to figure out what he wasn't saying. Taking a moment, he studied her face. Same dark golden skin, and liquid brown eyes he remembered. But the bright smile he'd seen their last morning together was replaced by pursed lips. She seemed fragile now in a way she hadn't been when they first met. He put on his stoic face, which he knew was damn good.

Stacey pulled out her phone. "I think the lobster one is usually around here today."

He raised his brows. "Lobster?"

"Yeah, they've got a killer roll. If you're not allergic, you totally need to try it. Woohoo! It is. They're a couple blocks away, but only for another hour. You should go get in line now."

"Thanks."

"You are so totally welcome. The wedding's on August nine-teenth. I'll let Hilda and Erin know you're coming."

"Hilda and Erin?"

"The brides. I introduced them." She had the smuggest grin going on. Which raised his hackles, as it would on any healthy, red-blooded, unattached-and-happy-with-it male. From the tensing of Radhika's body, she knew that grin well.

The elevator dinged and the doors opened. He placed his arm across the sensor for the people getting off and then gestured for Stacey and Radhika to get on. "What floor can I press for you?"

"Lobby's good for us. I have to escort Stacey out." Radhika glared at her friend. He had a feeling more than a few words would be passing between them once he was out of hearing range.

"Any pre-wedding events I should be aware of?"

"No."

"Yes."

Of course, it was Radhika who denied it. Stacey reached into her purse and dug around. She pulled out a ratty business card. "Here. Email me and I'll get back to you. I'm officially the maid of honor, though I'm not quite sure for which of them."

He took it and stuffed it into his back pocket. "Thanks." The doors opened and he couldn't resist stirring a little shit. "Radhika, I'll email you about the party. My sister's really excited to meet you."

He was halfway across the lobby when he heard Stacey's high-pitched squeal, "Sister?"

When he was back at his desk, he made a note to thank Stacey for the recommendation as the lobster roll had been phenomenal. He opened his email program and replied to a few that needed only quick responses.

There was a message from Bella saying she was sorry their meeting was cut short, and she looked forward to rescheduling. He narrowed his eyes. She probably didn't want anything in writing, but he'd be more careful around her in the future. He put that in the folder to respond to by the end of the day when he had more patience to craft a diplomatic letter about potentially stealing one of her staff.

Colm broke off from responding to a request for a class visit when he heard a knock on his door. It was the reporter Radhika was working with.

"Hey, Lee. What's up?"

"I hear you're possibly putting together a team for a project."

The gossip game in this office was strong. Colm picked up a pen from his desk and leaned back in his chair. "Yeah, but you're not a meteorologist."

"No, I'm here to make a case for Radhika."

Colm tamped down his immediate reaction. "I see. Why?"

"I like her. Oh, not like that, man. She's one of the best producers we have, but Bella is killing her. In fact, the reason I'm here is because I happened to be talking to Bella's assistant when she came back from lunch. She was on the phone as soon as she closed the door."

"So?"

"She was calling Dean."

Fuck. The network's bureau chief for DC was not a man to mess with. "Why?"

"Something about Radhika. Her door muffled most of what she said, but her assistant and I both clearly heard her say Dean and Radhika's names. If you've got any pull, you need to get Radhika away from that bitch."

"Whoa. What's going on here?"

"I have no clue. Bella's tough on all the producers, but she cuts the time on stories Radhika's producing all the damn time. Radhika then tells whichever reporter the story belongs to and we claw back some of the time. Never all of it, though. We all know it's Bella who's the problem. We've taken our complaints up top, but nothing's happened."

"I'll see what I can do." He worried more about burning a bridge, but from the sounds of this and his own personal experience, as short as it was, this bridge hadn't been that sturdy to begin with.

"Thanks, man. Oh, and welcome to DC. Let me know if you need tips on anything."

"Thanks, I will. How long have you been here?"

"Born and raised."

"Really?"

Lee had relaxed enough to grin. "Yeah, there is a thing called a DC native. Talk with you later."

"Later, man."

Colm rubbed the back of his neck. He'd need to carefully craft his approach to Dean. Though, if Lee was right, this might be something of a solution for Dean as well.

He picked up his phone and called Dean's assistant. Instead of forcing him to make an appointment, he was put right through.

"Colm. How are you doing?"

"Hey, Dean. I'm fine."

"Great. What can I do for you?"

Colm closed his eyes and focused his thoughts. He needed to leave Lee out of this so nothing blew back on him. "I was calling to touch base on the team project I want to do."

"The story about global warming and what Congress is doing and not doing, right?"

"Yeah."

"Sure, what about it?"

"I think I found the main producer I want to bring on. I was going to speak with her boss about it today, but something came up that cut our meeting short. Since then, I realized I probably should have run it by you first."

"Who?"

Colm heard the tension infuse Dean's tone and knew his boss had an idea as to who he was interested in. "Radhika O'Leary."

The other end of the line stayed quiet so long that Colm began to wonder if he'd been cut off. "O'Leary?"

"Yeah. Is that a problem?"

"Not a problem in the least. In fact, why don't you come up and we can discuss this further right now."

Colm glanced at his watch. He'd need to stay late tonight to finish the rest of the stuff he was working on, but, hell, you didn't say no to Dean. "Will do."

He only hoped Radhika didn't hate him forever for going behind her back like this.

3

*R*adhika sipped her beer as she and Jorie sat in the back of the bar across the street from the theater. The walls were lined with a combination of theater posters and signed headshots. The atmosphere still managed to give off a bit of a dive bar experience, unlike the upstairs which catered more toward the hipster crowd. Jorie was relaxed against the back of the bench seat as she sipped from her own bottle. Radhika envied the easy way Jorie could turn a moto jacket, T-shirt, and black jeans into what appeared to be high fashion, even with her tightly-curled brown hair pulled off her face with an elastic band as if she were going running instead of out for the night. She leaned in so Jorie could hear her question. "Should we pull her off him?"

Jorie studied the couple slow dancing a few feet away even though the music playing was some eighties hair metal band. "Nah. If this works out, she could use a good lay. It's been too long and she's getting on my nerves."

Stacey managed to suck half of the guy's tongue into her mouth. Both Radhika and Jorie looked at each other and made eww faces. "This is going to be a coyote ugly morning for her."

"More power to her." Jorie held up her beer bottle and Radhika clinked her own against it. "Tell me more about the

Hurricane Hottie. Stacey told me she met him at the station yesterday."

"Can you guys please call him Colm?"

Jorie sat there and mulled it over. "Nope. I like saying Hurricane Hottie."

"Am I being called?"

Radhika squeaked in surprise and looked up. "What are you doing here?"

"Stacey invited me." Colm grinned down at her.

She wanted to fume at her friend, but she kept getting distracted by Colm. A man should not look that hot in worn jeans and a royal blue Henley that made his eyes look even more delicious, and...was he really wearing cowboy boots? In DC? He smiled down at Jorie. "Hi, I'm Colm Jones."

Jorie smiled up at him and then back at Radhika, for whom it turned decidedly satanic. "Oh, I am *so* pleased to meet you. I'm Jorie."

"Are you another one of Radhika's friends?"

Jorie scooched over and patted the bench of the booth next to her. "One of her *best* friends."

"Not right now, you aren't."

"Hush up or I'll send you over there to break up the lovebirds."

"You're mean."

"Vicious, and don't you forget it."

"So, Jorie, how do you know Radhika?"

"Oh, we're a unit. Her, me, Stacey over there, who I think you've met?"

"I have."

"Well, the three of us and Hilda, and sometimes Erin, who is Hilda's fiancée."

"Why only sometimes?"

"Because Erin didn't get puked on."

Colm sat back on the bench. "Excuse me?"

"We all took a spin class together and sometimes hung out afterward. Well, this one class we had a new instructor who made my basic training drill sergeants look like balls of fluff.

Radhika there damn near fell off her bike at the end. The three of us were helping her out when she puked all over us. Projectile."

Colm bent to look around Jorie at her. "Really?"

Radhika shrugged her shoulders. "Not my finest moment. But we bonded."

"Over puke. Some people have blood brothers. We have the puke sisters."

"I wish you would stop calling us that. It's disgusting."

Colm started laughing.

"Laugh it up, Hurricane Hottie. I've been trying to get them to call you by your name, but if you don't stop, I'm not going to bother with that anymore."

Colm waved his hand and continued chuckling. Their waitress came over to see if they wanted any refills. Radhika and Jorie looked over at Stacey who was still sucking face with the dude. "Yeah, we'll take another round. Colm, do you want anything?"

He shook his head. "Thanks, but not right now. My brother-in-law is meeting me here. I mentioned to my sister I was going to stop by here and she kicked him out for the night so she could have her friends over to watch some show together."

Radhika checked her phone. "This late?"

He pulled out his own phone and set it on the table. "I'm sure my sister is lying and is trying to get us to bond more."

"How long has she been married to him?"

"Four years. He's a great guy, but I haven't spent much time alone with him since I haven't made it back here that often aside from work. Personally, I think we've bonded just fine and he'd probably say the same, but neither of us want to say anything to my sister."

Jorie was already shaking her head. "Yeah, you don't want to cross that line."

Colm's phone began flashing and he picked it up. "Yeah? What? I can barely hear you. Hang on."

He waved to them and they waved back as he headed upstairs to the ground floor of the bar.

Jorie nudged Radhika in the ribs with her elbow. "Serious hottie."

"Grow up."

"Never."

Stacey stumbled back over to them, the guy she'd been kissing nowhere to be seen. "Was that Colm I saw?"

"Yeah, he got a phone call. You shouldn't have invited him."

"Aw, isn't that sweet that he's here?"

Radhika looked at both of them. "No."

Stacey frowned. "Why not?"

"Because I wasn't the one who invited him."

Stacey shrugged her shoulders as she bumped hips with Radhika to make room. "Where did he go?"

Jorie took a pull of her beer before answering. "To meet someone."

Stacey got all mama bear, her back up and arms on the table, elbows locked. "A woman?"

Radhika glared at Jorie. "No. His brother-in-law, I think."

Ruffled fur soothed, she sat back in the booth. "Okay, that's fine. What did you guys think of the play?"

Jorie looked at Radhika and Radhika stared right back at her. Neither of them wanted to be the first to say it.

"It sucked, didn't it?"

"No. It didn't suck. It was interesting, that's all."

"It's that bitch Melissa's fault. She got a call this afternoon for a spot on a sitcom and didn't even bother calling our director until she was at Reagan."

"That's tacky."

Stacey's arms waved in the air. "Beyond tacky. You don't drop a play, no matter how small it is, just because Hollywood calls. First off, we've got contracts. Bitch burned her bridges. She'd better hope they don't drop her ass on the cutting room floor."

The waitress came back with their bottles of beer. Radhika immediately passed hers over to Stacey and signaled to the waitress for another one. The waitress side-eyed Stacey. "Is she going to be okay?"

"Yeah. Her play opened tonight, the leading lady bailed, and the understudy apparently has a drug problem no one had caught until tonight. We've got her."

The waitress winced and patted Stacey's shoulder. "I'm sorry, honey. I'll get your next round on the house."

Stacey reached up and hugged her. "You are the sweetest ever. Thank you."

The waitress rolled her eyes at Radhika and Jorie. "No worries, honey. You wallow with your friends. But stay away from Jerry. He's a no-good horndog."

"Yeah, he wasn't the best kisser."

The waitress disentangled herself and headed back to the bar to get another beer for Radhika. When they all had a bottle, they lifted them and clinked. Jorie and Stacey looked at each other and giggled. "To the puke sisters."

Radhika only shook her head and ignored them. Out of the corner of her eye, she saw cowboy boots coming down the stairs. They were followed by another pair of jean-clad legs. Probably his brother-in-law. Colm saw them right away and waved. He said something to the man behind him and headed over.

"Hey, you got room for two more?"

Stacey stood up and yanked on Radhika's arm until she climbed out of the booth.

Radhika glared at her friend. "What?"

Stacey smiled at Colm. "You two should sit over there. Your brother-in-law can sit with us."

Colm took one look at her and then glanced back at Stacey. "Tonight's supposed to be about me and my brother-in-law bonding. According to my sister, that is."

Stacey's face fell, but before she could say anything, the other man came over. "Problem?"

"Nope. Marcus, this is Radhika O'Leary. We work together. Radhika, this is my brother-in-law, Marcus Jones."

Surprised, Radhika glanced between the two. Colm, whose pale skin rivaled that of her Irish relatives, and Marcus whose skin was a dark brown. "Jones?"

Colm laughed. "Yeah, my sister was glad that she didn't have to do any of the paperwork related to changing her name."

Marcus smiled at them. "I'm pretty sure that was part of my appeal for her."

"Nice to meet you, Marcus. These are my friends, Jorie Douglas and Stacey Hardwicke."

"Ladies."

Jorie and Stacey both held out their hands to shake his. Jorie moved over. "Feel free to sit. Stacey's trying to play matchmaker with Radhika and Colm."

Marcus turned to look at them, a curious expression on his face. "Oh, really?"

"Jorie, can I see you in the bathroom for a moment? You, too, Stace?"

"Nope. Don't got to pee."

"Jorie."

"Why, Radhika, do you not want me to embarrass you in front of your new friends?"

"You are evil."

"I thought we settled this. Vicious."

Radhika sighed, knowing that whatever happened tonight was completely out of her control. Stacey climbed back into the booth and Radhika followed. Colm dragged a chair over from a nearby table and sat on the end, a little closer to Radhika than Marcus. She beat back the thrill she felt at that when she'd realized what he'd done. Stacey picked up the beer in front of her and paused. "Wait, is this my beer?"

Radhika grabbed the beer in front of her and switched it out for the one in Stacey's hand. "There's yours."

Stacey leaned over and kissed her cheek. "Thank you. I need to keep this drunk going."

Radhika shook her head, but caught the waitress's eye and signaled for her to come over. Colm and Marcus put in orders for beers from a local small-batch brewery that had an exclusive with the bar. It turned out one of the owners of the brewery was a coworker of Marcus's. "They're going into their third year and he's starting to talk about leaving our office as they're starting to get more orders than they can handle in their current space."

Radhika studied the label, committing it to memory. "That's great."

"It really is, but if he goes, I'll miss him. He's one of the best coders we have on staff."

Jorie leaned in. "Talk to him about doing some freelance work. He might be grateful to have a diversified income stream."

Marcus rubbed his chin. "I just might. Expansions can cost and I know he's trying to minimize the amount of debt they take on."

Colm leaned into Radhika and she shivered at the feeling of him so close, even if he was fully clothed. "Are you guys out celebrating or something? Stacey's email only said that you'd be here and I was welcome to join you."

"Stacey's play opened tonight. It's the first one she's authored that's been produced."

Colm leaned around her and clinked his bottle against Stacey's. "Congratulations!"

She looked confused for a moment and then grinned and clinked her bottle back. "Thanks."

He sat back and stretched his arm along the back of the bench. He wasn't touching her, but the feeling of being enclosed by his heat brought back delicious memories.

They spent another twenty minutes chatting until Marcus pulled his phone out of his pocket. He smiled and answered. "Hey, baby. Yeah, sure. Colm's here. Okay. See you in fifteen." He returned the phone to his back pocket and stood up. "Sorry, ladies, Colm. Kari wants me to stop at the store on the way home. My daughter's got a bit of a fever, and they've cut their TV night short."

They all made consoling noises and Colm stood as well. His fingers brushed against the back of her neck as he did so. Radhika shivered. Watching him, she couldn't tell if it had been a deliberate move or not. Probably not, but she had the sudden urge to fan herself. Colm and Marcus did some complicated male parting ritual and Marcus headed out. Colm glanced at the three of them and smiled. "While I'd love to stay later and have all of you to myself, I have to head out as well. See you tomorrow afternoon, Radhika."

She waved. "Anything I should bring?"

"Just yourself, but if there's some drink you particularly like, some of that."

"All right. See you tomorrow."

He strolled over to the bar and had a conversation with the waitress. She cashed him out and he signed the slip. He waved to them once more before heading up the stairs.

Both Jorie and Stacey waved their hands in front of their faces. It was Jorie who spoke first. "Hurricane Hottie indeed. He can blow me away anytime."

Radhika glared at her. "Jorie."

"What? I'm only stating the truth. As soon as you're done with him, pass him over my way."

"If you weren't all the way over there..."

Jorie smiled and waved at the waitress to get her attention. "What? You'd kick my ass? Good luck with that."

While Jorie had been out of the military for a few years now, she'd kept her fitness up. If you were walking down a dark alley at night, it was Jorie you'd want at your back. The waitress got another round for them, and when she delivered their drinks, she asked, "This is a fresh start. Want me to still split the tabs?"

They all froze. Radhika was the first to put the pieces together. "Did he pick up all of our tabs?"

"Yep, except for the one round of writer girl's here that was on the house. Nice guy."

"Yeah. He is. Thanks. If you could split them, that would be great."

She nodded and headed back to the bar. The three of them shared a look. Their bills hadn't exactly been cheap. When they'd first arrived, they'd done a couple of shots in celebration, and had kept the buzz going with the beer. Stacey was the first to break the silence. "You need to keep that one."

"He's not mine."

Stacey and Jorie glanced at each other and then turned their gazes on Radhika. They both burst into laughter. "He is dangling on your hook. He's yours if you want him."

"Please. We slept together once."

Stacey's arched look was worthy of being on one of those period British shows.

"Fine. Two nights. That's it. If he'd wanted it to be more, he could have called me. I bet he's been bed-hopping his way across the country since."

Jorie leaned forward. "Tell Dr. Jorie all about it. Were you put out that he didn't call?"

"No! No. I'm an adult and I could have called him, too, if I wanted. I didn't."

Stacey rested her chin on her hand. "Why didn't you?"

"Because it was a one-night stand." Of course, the music would cut out at just that moment. She glanced around, but the other bar patrons had the grace to ignore her.

Probably giving thanks to whatever god they worshipped it hadn't been them caught in the silence. She turned back to her friends and lowered her voice. "It was supposed to be a one-night stand. I'm an adult. I'm allowed to have them."

Jorie shrugged. "Hell, anyone can have them. But, I have never seen a man that casually affectionate with someone he views only as a former one-night stand. And what's this about meeting his sister?"

Radhika blew out a breath. "I'm acting as his beard."

"That man is far from gay." Stacey lifted her beer to sip and realized both of her friends were staring at her. "What? You can always tell. Can't you?"

Both Jorie and Radhika shook their heads. Stacey shrugged. "Maybe it's a theater thing. I can tell, and I have yet to be wrong. So, since he's not gay or bi, you are not his beard."

Radhika rubbed her eyes. "I'm his beard in the sense that this is a platonic date. His sister insisted he have one because she doesn't want the friends she invited sniffing around him." Jorie and Stacey stared at her. "That's what he told me!"

Jorie reached over and patted her hand. "You go on believing that."

Radhika initiated a tiny slap fight with Jorie and then sipped her beer. "I will. In fact, I'm going to ask his sister tomorrow if I get a chance."

Stacey tapped her arm with the beer bottle. "Tell me again why you deigned to whine about Vince leaving you after getting some of that?"

Radhika slumped down in the booth. "Because I'm a brain-dead idiot who barely learns from her mistakes."

Jorie and Stacey narrowed their eyes. It was Jorie who reached over the table and gripped Radhika's arm. "Vince was an asshole who didn't know the best thing in his life from a hole in the ground. Yes, he was an absolute dick in leading you on to think he was about to propose to you. You're better off without him."

Even well over a year later, Radhika still felt the gut punch when he announced in front of all their coworkers that he appreciated her help in making him look good for the higher ups, but he had to break up with her and move on. "I'm done. No more coworkers. No more news guys. Hell, no more guys who are prettier than they ought to be."

Stacey scrunched her face up. "So, one-night stands are okay, but relationships aren't?"

Radhika stared at her beer bottle. "Yep."

adhika walked out of the Metro stop and consulted her phone for directions to Colm's sister's house. She'd put off coming until after five, but with track work delays, she'd had to wait over fifteen minutes for a train. If Colm's sister and Marcus had lived farther from the station, she'd have gotten a taxi, but as they were only a few blocks away, the walk didn't seem too bad.

Plus, she wanted to stop at one of the specialty liquor stores in the area before heading over so she could grab a couple of bottles of her favorite wine. Rory had snatched the last one for his night in with Cecilia.

There were few people in the store, so she was able to get the wine and then to the house in short order, even strolling along and studying the mixture of row houses, duplexes, and single-family homes. Colm's sister and Marcus lived in one of the single-family homes and the exterior looked to be recently painted with light blue paint on the siding and dark green and black accents. Standing outside the closed door, she could hear loud voices and laughter coming through it. She started to knock and realized she may not be heard.

It took a while, but she found the doorbell. Chimes rang inside. A couple of minutes later, the door opened and a woman about her height with Colm's coloring stood there. She smiled and pushed open the screen door as a toddler with the chubbiest cheeks ran up and stood behind her. "Hi, you must be Radhika. I'm Kari, Colm's sister."

"Nice to meet you." The toddler was waving madly, so Radhika bent down and held out her hand. "And who is this?"

The little girl turned shy and buried her face into Kari's leg. Kari reached down and brushed her hand over the girl's hair. "This is my daughter, Nya. Can you say hi, Nya?"

Radhika heard a distinct "hi" even though it was muffled by the jeans Kari wore. Kari rolled her eyes and picked up Nya, settling her into the crook of one arm. "Come on in. Most of the party is in the kitchen or out on our back deck. Can I get you something to drink?"

Radhika pulled out one of the bottles of wine. "Here, this is for you. Thanks for inviting me."

Kari smiled and then saw the label and her eyes widened. "Wow. Thank you. This is one of Marcus's favorites."

"It's mine, too. I grabbed a few extra bottles to bring home."

Kari grinned. "Don't let Marcus near your bag, then. He'd pay you back, but I'd bet the store will be closed before you leave here and I'd hate for you to make another trip out if you didn't have to."

Colm came in at that moment. He was dressed in shorts and a shirt that molded to damn near every muscle of his shoulders and chest. "Kari, where are the kabobs? Oh, Radhika. Glad you're here." He walked over and gave Radhika a quick hug before he kissed the back of his niece's head. She should not be jealous of a toddler. She did not want those lips on her again. Nope. Not at all.

"They're in the fridge where I told you they were last time."

"Your friends are hungry pigs, so you know."

"Why do you think I prepped so much food and told them to bring their own?"

He headed back into the kitchen and Radhika watched the athletic grace of his body as Kari shook her head. "That boy."

"I thought you were only a year older?"

"I am, but it's like he goes back to age twelve and helpless when I'm around."

Radhika laughed. "My brother does the same, but he's seven years younger than me."

Kari shifted Nya in her arms. "Any in between?"

"No. Just me and Rory."

"Since you're an older sister, I hope you'll appreciate that I insisted Colm bring a date or a friend with him."

Radhika's brows rose. "I was going to ask you about that if I had a chance. He was serious about that?"

"As a heart attack. I love my friends, but a hornier bunch, you will never meet. And most of them are single for whatever reason right now. Marcus and I invited some of our single coworkers and other friends to give Colm a bit of cover, but I figured if he had a friend of his own it would be another layer of protection."

"Wow. I've never had to be that protective of Rory, and he was voted homecoming king in high school."

"Yeah, that photo spread of Colm's is all my friends have been able talk about for the last couple of months. They started asking when he'd be visiting next, and when they found out he was moving here? Rabid. Downright rabid. I think some of them were glad there was going to be someone around who was single, good looking, and not part of the politics pool."

Radhika thought back to some of the dates she'd had when she first moved to the area and winced. "I can understand."

Kari's laugh was throaty and full. "I think all of us who've spent any time single in DC can. Let's get some food into you. Colm told you not to have dinner, right?"

Radhika smiled, enjoying the easy friendliness of this woman. "I figured there'd be food since he told me the party started in the afternoon. I'm sorry I'm late, by the way."

"No worries. There are a few other stragglers who had overlapping plans. We tend to hang out in the backyard drinking and watching a fire late into the night, so things are pretty free flowing around here."

Radhika set her bag down in a pile that had accumulated

outside of the kitchen entrance. "Is there anything I can do to help?"

Kari looked over her shoulder. "You're from the Midwest, aren't you?"

"Yeah, how can you tell?"

"Almost all of you walk in for the first time and ask if you can help. There's the odd one that fakes me out, but everyone who asks is from somewhere in the Midwest. What part are you from?"

"Minnesota. Bloomington."

Kari set Nya down and the little girl immediately ran over to the fridge and tried to open it. Kari followed, and pulled a plastic tube from the door. She tore the top off and handed it to her daughter who started sucking on it. "I'm not familiar with Minnesota outside of Minneapolis and St. Paul."

"We're one of the southern suburbs."

"How long have you been in DC?"

"About ten years now."

"Nice. Do live in DC?"

"Yeah. I've got a condo over near Nats Park."

"Wow. Nice."

Radhika leaned a hip against the island in the kitchen and ran her hand over the marble. "I managed to get in while they were building, and my parents helped a little so I could get a two-bedroom. That way I'd have a guest room for their use when they came to visit."

Kari laughed and pulled a few more things from the fridge. "Smart people."

"Yeah. My brother moved here to go to school for a while, but ended up dropping out. He's now in the second bedroom."

"Better with older sis than back at home?"

"That's what Mum said. They love us, but they're also greatly enjoying being empty nesters."

"What about losing access to the guest room?"

Radhika grinned. "When they come to town, Rory gets kicked out to the couch in the living room."

"I appreciate the way your parents operate."

The kitchen door to the backyard opened and this time it was Marcus who came in. "Hey, babe."

"Dada."

Marcus bent down and scooped up Nya in his arms before she could plaster herself and her tube of yogurt all over him. "Hey, baby girl. Mommy get you some yogurt?" Nya nodded as she continued sucking on the tube. "Good. We got any burgers left, babe?"

"Some." She turned to Radhika. "What would you like? We've got chicken kabobs that have been marinating in Italian dressing. There's also burgers and brats."

"Anything vegetarian?"

"We were saving them in case anyone asked, but we've got Portobello mushrooms that we can grill up and there's some veggie kabobs out there, too."

"That'd be perfect. Thanks."

Kari went back to the fridge and dug a sealed pack of Portobello mushrooms out of one of the drawers. "Babe, would you take Nya outside and give her to Colm? I'll be out with these in a little bit."

"Sure. Good to see you again, Radhika."

"You, too, Marcus."

He headed back out and Radhika went over to help Kari. "I can skin those. Do you have any olive oil?"

Thankful the gills and stems had already been removed, she peeled the thin outer skins off and Kari came back with a narrow bottle of green liquid. "What kinds of spices do you have?"

"Salt, pepper, a whole lot of others. Marcus likes things flavorful."

"I'll take the salt and pepper. What about paprika and cumin?"

"I'll be right back." Kari came back with a selection of spices and Radhika prepped the mushrooms.

Kari handed her a plate. "If you want to take those out, Marcus will put them on the grill. He's made them before, so he knows what he's doing."

"I never had any doubts." She headed into the backyard and immediately saw why Kari had insisted on Colm bringing a date. There were four women who had circled him. He had Nya in his arms, almost positioned as a shield. Sadly, a hot man with cute little girl in his arms did nothing to deter females like that. What did help was said cute little girl wasn't letting anyone get between her and her uncle. She'd attached herself to Colm's neck and wasn't letting go, the nearly empty yogurt tube hanging from her mouth. Colm was even slightly rocking as if she were an infant.

Radhika walked over to where Marcus was flipping burgers, brats, and kabobs on the grill. He saw her walking over and smiled.

"Set them down right there." He pointed at a staging table to his right with the flipper. "The coolers with beer and liquor are over on there on the right, and the two on the left have water and soft drinks. Pick your poison."

"Thanks." She glanced over at Colm and Nya. "Kari told me she wanted him to have a date as a shield. Should I go save him?"

Marcus studied the group and grinned. "Yeah, he can come work the grill. They'll try to follow him over here, but you stick with him and Kari will be out in a minute to make sure they circulate."

"All righty." She went over to one of the coolers first and picked out a bottle of Guinness. She popped the cap off and observed the group. Colm kept inching back, and the women kept following. If he wasn't careful, he'd trip over one of the occupied chairs in a minute. She worked her way around the other groups and came up behind Colm. Thanks to his height, and good looks, the women were distracted until Radhika showed up next to him. She placed her hand on his back so he wouldn't jump and drop Nya.

He glanced down, saw it was her, and grinned. After shifting Nya into his other arm, he wrapped his newly free one around Radhika's shoulders. It was if someone had snapped next to her ear and everything clicked into place. She had the irrational urge to snuggle in until no air could pass between them. "Ladies, this is Radhika O'Leary. Radhika, these are my sister's friends."

They were all watching the placement of his arm, and varying levels of frowns and sour expressions formed. Radhika gave them her friendliest smile. "Nice to meet you all. The weather's gorgeous today for a party."

The one immediately to her left ignored her opening gambit and went for the throat. "How do you know Colm? He's never mentioned you to us, and neither has Kari."

Radhika smiled up at Colm and patted his chest. Nya reached out and patted her hand and she winked at the little girl. "We've known each other for a while. Both of us work at the network."

One of the other women's perfectly drawn brows arched up. "Oh? What is it that you do? I've never seen you on TV."

Radhika recognized that tone and let her smile grow a little hard as she stared the woman in the eyes until her gaze shifted off to the side. "I'm a producer. Not all of us want to be in front of the camera." *Smooth, O'Leary. Very smooth.* "Colm, Marcus asked me to come get you. He wants a break from the grill for a bit."

He rubbed her shoulder. "Thanks. See you ladies later. It was good catching up with you."

The three of them walked over to where Marcus stood. Out of the corner of her eye, she saw two of the women try to follow, but Kari had come outside and shepherded them back into the larger group. Marcus was rubbing his mouth, and Radhika could see that he was hiding a grin.

He handed the flipper over to Colm and took his daughter. "It's all yours, my brother."

They fist bumped, and Colm did the same with Nya. She held out her tiny fist to Radhika and she bumped it with her own. The little girl giggled as Marcus carried her away to talk to one of the guys who was hanging on the edges of the group. Colm checked everything on the grill and closed the lid. "Your mushrooms will be ready soon. Kari's got a spread with plates, utensils, sides, buns, and condiments over by the house if you want to get some."

"Thanks, I'll be right back."

The spread was comprehensive, and Radhika felt like she was back in her old neighborhood when massive parties were held at people's houses just because it was a nice night to be out grilling. She prepped a bun with the fixings and loaded the rest of her plate with a variety of sides.

The woman who'd done the polite sneer at her not being on TV was hanging around the grill, and when Radhika got closer, the woman reached out and stroked Colm's biceps. *Please, bitch.* She cleared her throat when she got closer and Colm jumped. He reached out and dragged her closer, under his arm. She had to juggle her plate so she didn't drop anything either on the ground or down Colm's front. She was supposed to be his fake date, but he was certainly acting as if their relationship was a lot deeper than that of coworkers or a former one-night stand.

What would it be like to be his steady girlfriend? Not that it was a possibility, because she was done with dating coworkers. Maybe if she kept reminding herself, it would sink in. He looked down at her, and she would have sworn there was a glimmer of panic in his eyes. "You ready for your dinner?"

Radhika held up her plate. "All set."

He opened the grill, staying as far from the woman as possible, and scooped out one of the mushrooms, putting it on her bun. "Tracy, I think Kari's waving for you."

Both Tracy and Radhika glanced over and Kari was indeed pointing at them and motioning to come back. "Oh, maybe she wants to give Radhika a seat so she can eat. I can keep you company."

Radhika narrowed her eyes. "That's sweet of her, but I'm good. Colm and I have some things to discuss about work, anyway."

Tracy didn't back down. "You shouldn't turn down a hostess's offer of a seat. That's not being a good guest."

Damn. Tracy had some serious cojones. Radhika gave Tracy her sweetest smile. "You're absolutely right." She started to head over, but Kari obligingly started waving her arms in the air in the universal sign of no and pointed emphatically at Tracy.

Radhika looked back at the other woman. "It looks like she meant you. And I know you'd hate to be a poor guest."

Radhika imagined she heard Tracy's teeth grinding, but the woman headed back to where Kari was sitting.

Colm let out a low breath. "Thanks. I've had it with predatory women this week."

Radhika bit into her mushroom burger and chewed as she watched Kari talk very heatedly in Tracy's ear. "She wasn't too bad."

Colm rubbed the back of his neck. "After dealing with Bella a few days ago, I would just like to be left alone."

Radhika took a step back. "Bella?"

"Yeah. I wasn't going to tell you since she's your boss and all, but she was coming on to me pretty strong in the cafeteria the other day. That's why I cut our meeting short."

She reached out and rubbed his bicep. After a few moments, she felt the tension coiled there lessen a little bit. Not much, but some. "I'm sorry."

"Nothing for you to be sorry about. She's an adult who should know how to behave better."

Radhika snorted. "There's a lot she should know how to do better, but that doesn't mean she does." She took another bite of the mushroom burger.

"I'm beginning to wish I'd never agreed to be a part of that magazine spread."

"Only now?"

"Yeah. It was amusing at first, but it's old now."

"Why did you agree then?"

"My agent. She thought it would be good exposure and a negotiating tool. I'd been considering looking for a job up here."

Radhika watched as Marcus walked over to where Kari was sitting with her friends. Nya dropped down out of his arms, but she could see this was something the family had done often as neither parent was surprised by the move and smoothly passed control from one to the other. Marcus bent down and kissed Kari on the lips as Nya settled herself in Kari's lap. He headed back to his buddy he'd been talking with earlier. She felt a tug in her heart, and a low hum of want. The easy trust between partners was something she'd never truly experienced. "You wanted to spend more time with your family?"

"Yeah. Nya's at the age where she appreciates me being around, and I haven't been able to spend more than a few days here and there hanging out with Kari and Marcus. Don't get me wrong, I've loved all of the travel and it's not like we didn't do it often as kids."

Radhika looked up at him, but his attention was back on the grill as he moved the meats and kabobs that were done onto platters. She waited for him to finish fussing. "Why did you travel so much as kids?"

"Dad was a corporate executive. Well, first he was on a troubleshooting team, but he was good enough that he went up through the ranks."

"Like a military brat without the military."

"You got it. Kari and I got to see a lot of the world, and we were in Asia for some massive typhoons. That's what got me interested in meteorology. At first, I thought I'd go to work for Dad's company, but he was the one who encouraged me to explore broadcasting. He said I was good at explaining things." He grinned. "I was hooked with my first test broadcast."

"I'm surprised you keep up the travel. A lot of people I know who've had nomadic lifestyles as kids tend to plant roots and not move."

He nodded over to Kari. "That's my sister. She came out to UMD for college and hasn't left. She didn't hook up with Marcus until a few years ago, but she hasn't left the area. I haven't found a place that particularly feels like home to me, so I keep moving."

"Are you planning on staying in the area?"

He shrugged. "For a few years, at least. My current contract is with the network at large, so I can change home locations if I need to. There's been talk about pulling me up to New York, but DC's a decent compromise for now. If they need me up there, it's a quick trip."

Radhika mulled that over as she finished the burger and

began picking at the salads and sides she'd picked up. "I know a lot of people who'd kill to be in the NYC offices. Why not you?"

He shrugged again. "New York's a nice place to visit, but I've never felt all that comfortable up there. Commuting can be a bitch, and, frankly, I can't stand the trash that they stick out on the sidewalks."

"No alleys."

"No, but they could still find a better way than to put the trash out where people are walking, even if they manage to leave that until later in the night."

Radhika tilted her head to study him. "I wouldn't have taken you to be so fastidious."

"Why not? According to the magazine, I'm *a perfectly polished specimen of manhood.*"

Radhika almost choked on the corn and pepper salad. "What you are is a frat boy in disguise."

He stepped back with one hand on his heart and the other pointing the burger flipper at her. "You take that back. I was never a frat boy."

"Why? Too pretty for them?"

He went back to checking the food on the grill. "Nah. Too geeky and I didn't have enough time for it with double majoring."

"You? A geek?"

Only his eyes turned toward hers, but she could read the pity in them. "All of us in the meteorology program were geeky. Even if we were good looking enough to end up on TV." He winked. "It also helped that I had no problem getting dates on my own."

Radhika rolled her eyes at him, but he only laughed and shouted for Marcus to come over and man the grill again. Then he led her over to a lightly populated set of chairs. He told her to sit and that he'd be right back. He was, with two bottles of beer and a plate full of food. He passed one bottle to her. "So, tell me what J-school was like for you."

5

*C*olm enjoyed listening to Radhika talk. She'd made him laugh earlier with the way she'd stood up to the four terrors. He'd met his sister's friends on and off over the years, but they'd never been so...insistent. Even Tracy who'd periodically hit on him a few times while in relationships, hadn't been so aggressive.

Things had been relatively light before Radhika showed up. They had probably been waiting for him to show a preference for one of them. Then Radhika came and they must have decided to band together to oust the outsider. Like he'd ever date or sleep with one of his sister's friends. He hadn't even done that in high school. And they'd been at a small boarding school for most of those years. Thank God they'd gone to separate colleges.

He stretched his arms over his head as he watched Marcus and one of his friends build up the fire. It had finally gotten dark and cool enough, so everyone had pulled their chairs in closer. A couple of Kari's friends had already bailed, but Tracy and the other one were still there. They were sitting across from him and Radhika, whispering to each other and periodically looking over at them.

Colm avoided catching their eye, but he was smart enough

not to completely ignore them. Any time Radhika had gone into the house to use the bathroom or whatever, Kari or one of the other ladies at the party had gone in with her. Tracy and the crew had left her alone for the most part, but there was enough of a mean-girl vibe about them that he wouldn't trust them even half as far as he could throw them. He still wondered why Kari kept them around as friends.

Speaking of his sister, she came back outside after changing Nya into pajamas. His niece looked wiped, but she was also carrying a bag of marshmallows with her. Kari had a box of graham crackers and a pack of chocolate bars in her other hand. Apparently, Nya had managed to talk her way into some s'mores. All the better for him. Kari sat down next to Marcus handing him the crackers and chocolate, and he passed her a metal skewer with three ends.

Colm patted Radhika on the shoulder. He felt the muscles tense for a moment, then relax. The temptation to leave his hand there was great. Getting her to snuggle up to him when she'd first come outside had him feeling as if something clicked into place in his universe. Not the best thought to have when she had defined them as platonic friends only. "I'll be right back. Want some s'mores?"

She sat up and looked around. "Hell, yeah. Where?"

He laughed. "We've got to make them. Hold on."

Marcus looked up from the fire when he came over. Without even asking, he picked up and held out another skewer.

Colm took it. "Thanks."

"Give Kari a second to open the marshmallows."

"Got them." She passed over a handful to Colm and then plopped one on the skewer she held.

Colm walked back to Radhika and handed her the marshmallows. "How many do you want?"

"One at a time until I'm full or your sister and brother-in-law run out of supplies. If I'd known there was going to be a fire like this, I would have brought my stash as well."

"Love s'mores, do you?"

"They're one of my favorite desserts. I made sure that I would have a gas stove so I could make them in winter."

Colm paused in the middle of skewering the marshmallow he'd taken. "You made sure you had a gas stove just so you could make s'mores?"

"Sure. Wouldn't you?"

"S'mores are for making over a fire. The smoke adds flavor."

"S'mores over fires are the best, but if you can't build a fire in your condo, like I can't, a natural gas burner is the next best thing. Believe me, the last thing you want to make s'more over is a Sterno can. That leaves a foul taste."

He watched her as he handed over the skewer. "You still ate them, didn't you?"

"Yep." She was focused on roasting the marshmallow over the fire. Her technique was pristine. She didn't let any hot spots develop, and when the marshmallow appeared ready to catch fire, she blew it out. He always appreciated watching a master, no matter the skill. A small plate with graham crackers and chocolate bits made their way around the circle to them. Colm took more than a few and put them on the plate he'd cleaned earlier, but hadn't gotten around to throwing away yet. Radhika held out her hand. "Cracker."

He passed it to her with a piece of chocolate on it. She glanced down and nodded. She pulled the marshmallow, perfectly browned and sagging on the tongs of the skewer, back from the fire and placed it on top of the bottom half of the sandwich. He reached over with another cracker half and placed it on top of the marshmallow, holding it in place until she reconfigured her fingers to hold the sweet sandwich together as she pulled the skewer out. The glide of her fingers against his set heat coursing through his system. She scraped what melted mallow she could off onto the cracker and then handed him the skewer. "Thanks."

"It's a pleasure to watch a master at work."

"Girl Scouts. We know our s'mores."

"I thought you knew cookies."

"How do you think the cookie thing got started?" She bit

into the dessert and the look on her face wasn't that far from what he remembered when she orgasmed, and he'd seen that often enough in the two nights they'd spent together. He shifted in his seat as he felt his cock starting to fill. He turned back to the fire and focused on roasting his own marshmallow.

Radhika could have slapped him that first day and stayed far away, but she'd been professional, and he'd treated her the same way. He would have anyway, but still. They knew each other. Intimately. He blew out a breath. He needed to get a handle on this...whatever it was.

She swatted his arm.

"What?"

She pointed at the fire. "You're burning."

He was indeed. The marshmallow was a glorious briquette of carbonized sugar. He shouldn't read anything allegorical into this. It was burnt marshmallow, not the state of his love life. "Damn."

"Here, give it to me."

He passed her the skewer and the marshmallows. She picked up the fork that was sitting on his plate and used it to scrape the burned marshmallow off the tongs of the skewer. He sat back in the chair and watched her expertly roast a marshmallow for him.

"Do you want a dark or light crust?"

"Dark, but you don't have to cook it as long as I did."

The look she shot him over her shoulder was pure exasperation, but she turned back to the fire. He watched as light danced off the earrings she wore in her right ear. She only had two piercings on the left side, but on the right, they went halfway up her ear. He wondered how comfortable that was when she had to wear headphones. He had no piercings and some days those headsets were intolerable.

He leaned his head over until he heard a crack in his neck. Sitting out here with her, his family, and friends was supposed to be relaxing, but he felt keyed up all thanks to the woman next to him.

The guy to his right, one of Marcus's friends, nudged his side. "Hey, man. Got any marshmallows left?"

"Yeah. Need a skewer?"

"I'm good. Your niece started throwing the marshmallows from the bag into the fire, so what you've got is what's left."

Colm looked around the fire and saw that Kari and Nya were missing and that Marcus was heading back into the house. How on Earth had he missed that little drama?

He was sure Nya had probably screamed a few times when Kari would have attempted to stop her. His niece was a cutie pie, but she also wasn't afraid to make her feelings known if she felt she was being crossed. He reached over and plucked one of the marshmallows from the plate on Radhika's lap.

"Hey!"

"Emergency share. You've got the last of the stock."

She sighed, but didn't continue arguing. He'd bet after what she'd told him earlier that she had her own supply of ingredients back at her condo ready to go and would probably fire up her stove if she didn't get enough here. He passed it to the guy next to him. "Here you go...sorry, I forget your name."

"Jay."

Colm held out his hand and they shook. "What do you do?"

Jay looked at him for a moment. "Defense."

Colm recognized the universal-to-DC "don't ask anything more" answer. "Got it."

"How was the move up here?"

"Not bad. It helped to have Marcus around for the heavy lifting."

"He's good for that. He helped me a few times."

"How did you two meet?"

"I used to work for him when I was in college. We're still on a softball team."

"Cool."

"You play sports?"

"Not much. My schedule isn't the best for joining teams since I can't commit to being at every game."

"Feel free to come out when you're in town. I can guarantee we always need an extra body on hand."

"I will. Thanks."

Radhika elbowed him. "Cracker."

He set up the bottom with chocolate and held it out for her. She placed the perfectly roasted marshmallow on top of it and as he was about to put the top on, also layered with a piece of chocolate, she snatched the chocolate out and popped it in her mouth. "Hey."

"The price of me doing your work. Plus, you only gave me one piece for mine. Stop being greedy."

"You're ruthless."

She stared at him. "Oh, you think I'm going to try to deny that. Nope."

He laughed and bit into his s'more. The graham cracker, chocolate, and marshmallow perfectly blended on his tongue. It wasn't something he went for often, but tonight? It was almost the perfect ending to the evening. Radhika shifted in the chair next to him and pulled her phone out of her back pocket.

"Anything wrong?"

"No. Just a text from my brother. Though I wish he hadn't."

"Why? Where is he?"

"At home with his girlfriend."

"So?"

She stared at him for a moment. "We share the condo and he said it was okay to come home if I wanted to."

"Oh. *Ohhhh.*"

"Yeah. They've been together for over a year and I'd rather avoid having to think about that part of their relationship."

"Why don't they go to her place?"

"She lives with her parents in the suburbs."

"You are a nice older sister."

Radhika shrugged. "It helps that I really like Cecilia. Her parents are pretty cool, too, but they're religious and activities like that are not to even be thought of in their home."

"Fair enough."

"Yeah."

"How old are they?"

"Mid-twenties. Cecilia's got a new job and is looking at grad school. Rory, thank the gods, is considering going back to college for his Bachelor's. She's almost got him convinced. The problem is that he's still not sure what he wants to study."

"Is he having a problem growing up?"

"More that's he's interested in a lot of things, and school isn't one of them. The main reason we share the condo is because of the cost of living around here and our parents contribute a little to his share as long as he lives with me."

He debated asking the next question, but he couldn't hold it back. "Doesn't that get a little awkward when you're dating someone?"

She shrugged. "Not really. Some of the guys have had their own places, and most of them haven't been worth the logistics of figuring that out, so I never bothered."

He popped the last of his s'more into his mouth and chewed as he thought over his next question. "So, the hotel thing with me was a fluke."

She became totally still. He hadn't thought it possible of a human being, but she managed it. Then, she bent her head and her fingers started flying across her phone. "Yeah, it was. Remember, rebound?"

Still a bit uncomfortable about that admission, he only nodded and sat contemplating both her and the fire. She was the brighter of the two. He'd thought of her from time to time since their interlude, but when he'd been back in DC since then and was between relationships, it was usually for quick overnight visits or to specifically spend time with Kari, Marcus, and Nya.

He hadn't felt comfortable with the idea of arranging a booty call when he was supposed to be spending time with his niece. Radhika stood and stretched.

"Need something?"

"No, I'm going to head home. Thanks for inviting me over."

He reached out for her hand and tugged it. "Not yet."

"What do you mean, not yet?"

He pulled on her hand until she bent down closer to him. "Tracy and Missy are still here and I'm not ready to say goodbye to Kari and Marcus yet."

"How is that my problem?"

"You promised to be my fake date, remember."

Out of the corner of his eye, he saw Jay turn his head to them at that.

Radhika waved at him and then bent even closer so her lips were brushing against his ear. "Again, not my problem. Let go of my hand or lose your nuts."

He did as requested. Before she stood up, she kissed his cheek and said loudly enough so it carried to the other side of the fire. "Back in a bit."

As she sashayed into the house—and it was definitely a sashay—he watched as Tracy and Missy turned their heads to glare at Radhika's back. Yeah, no love lost there.

"Fake date?"

He turned to see Jay grinning at him. "So?"

"You that hard up, man?"

"No."

"So...she's available?"

"No!"

Jay held his hands up and sat back in his chair. "Just checking, man. We're cool."

Colm scrubbed his hands over his face. "Yeah, we are. Sorry."

"It's all right."

Kari came back outside, but there was no sign of Radhika.

She plopped down in the empty chair next to him. "Give serious thought to having kids of your own, little brother."

"I heard she was tossing the marshmallows into the fire pit."

"Yeah." She blew out a breath that ruffled the bangs that had fallen down the front of her face. "I was talking with Tracy and Marcus was talking to someone else, so neither of us noticed until she was about to throw the bag in. Dammit."

"Too bad she's not big enough to clean the pit out herself."

"She's damn lucky she isn't. As it is, Marcus is going to have to make sure none of that shit is caked onto the brick."

"Is she asleep?"

"Like an angel. Where did Radhika go?"

"Inside."

"I didn't see her in the kitchen."

"Maybe she was in the bathroom."

"Maybe. Shit. Back in a moment."

Kari got up and raced to the house. He realized why when he saw that the seats Tracy and Missy had been in were vacated. "Shit." He got up and went in, too.

He opened the door just in time to see Tracy step back a foot, hands on her hips as she faced Kari. Radhika was standing in the hallway, a sad look on her face. She saw Colm and waved. He asked if she was okay by mouthing the words and she nodded.

"Get the fuck out of my house, Tracy. You, too, Missy."

"What the hell, Kari? You're choosing that bitch over us?"

Colm had been edging around the kitchen to go to Radhika, but he caught sight of his sister's face and he immediately detoured to catch hold of her waist before she did something she'd regret.

"She's not the bitch standing in this kitchen. That's you two whores."

Whoa. What the hell had happened to turn his sister against her friends like this?

"Fuck you, Kari."

"Fuck you, you tasteless wench."

"Shit." Colm readjusted his grip as his sister started squirming.

Marcus came flying into the room, and halted just behind where Tracy was, smartly, leaning over the island to hurl insults at Kari. Missy was just standing off to the side looking stunned. Marcus stepped over toward Missy and cleared his throat. "What's going on here? We've got a sleeping kid upstairs."

Nya had perfect timing as she shouted down the stairs. "Mommy, Dada?"

Radhika raised a hand. "I'll go up." And then she scooted out of there.

"Kari?" Marcus looked between his wife and her two friends.

She shook herself out of Colm's grip. She was still pissed, but now he didn't fear that she would assault either of them. "Get them the fuck out of here, Marc. My baby needs me." She headed through the hallway Radhika had used to avoid having to go around Tracy or Missy.

Marcus looked at him, but he could only shrug his shoulders and lift his hands. "Ladies, my wife asked you to leave. Do I need to call a cab for you?"

Tracy sniffed and patted down her hair. "No. Missy drove over. She can drive me home."

And wouldn't that be a fun ride? He wasn't sure if Missy had been involved in whatever the hell set Kari off, but from the dirty look she shot Tracy, she wasn't having any of this. She did, however, immediately go over to where the bags had been set and grabbed hers. "I'm sorry, Marcus. Colm. Please tell Kari that."

"Missy, let's go."

Tracy flung open the door and stalked out. Missy blew out a breath and waved goodbye to them. She closed the door softly, but firmly. Through the open windows, he could hear them arguing as they walked to Missy's car.

Jay came in the back door. "Everything okay in here?"

"Yeah, we're good, man."

Jay watched Marcus and turned to Colm. "You okay?"

"I guess. I have no idea what happened."

Jay gave him a small smile. "I'm sure you'll hear about it. I'll let everyone outside know whatever happened has blown over."

"Thanks."

Colm thought about heading upstairs, but Nya didn't need any more adults crowding around in her room. He heard someone coming downstairs, and saw it was Radhika when she turned into the living room. She stopped by the pile of bags and picked up a backpack. "Where are you going?"

"Home. I should have left earlier."

He went over and rubbed her shoulders. The muscles there were coiled tight, but as he rubbed, he felt them slacken. "What happened?"

"I have no clue. I came out of the bathroom and Tracy and the other friend were standing in the kitchen waiting for me. I offered to help them clean up the kitchen if that's what they were doing. Tracy then said I had gall trying to claim her property and that I should dump you."

"What?"

"Yeah. That's when your sister came in and you saw what happened after that."

"What the ever-loving fuck?"

Radhika lifted her shoulders. "I guess my job for the night is done. I need to get to the Metro before they close, anyway."

"Screw that, I'll get a cab for you."

"No, thanks."

"Fine, I'll drive you."

"Colm, you're not listening. I'm going home. On my own. Via the mode of transportation that I choose."

"Radhika, I am so sorry." They turned to see Kari coming down the stairs. "I never thought they'd be like that."

"No, I'm sorry. You shouldn't have to talk to your friends like that."

"Exactly, which makes this in no way your fault. I don't know what the hell is going on with Tracy, and, frankly, I don't care." Radhika went over and hugged Kari who hugged her back. "Thanks. And, please, take Colm up on his offer. I'd rather know you got home safe after this."

"Well, okay." She looked over her shoulder at him. "Can we go now?"

"Of course." He walked over to the two of them and kissed Kari on the forehead. "I'll let you know when I've got her home and I'll call you tomorrow."

She nodded, then hugged him. "I'm sorry, Colm."

"Yeah, what guy doesn't like hearing that women are fighting over him?"

Kari slugged him in the shoulder, and, damn. He rubbed his shoulder. "What did Mom tell you about hitting me?"

"Only if you deserved it, and you know you deserved it."

He hugged her. "Tomorrow."

"Yeah. Bye, Radhika. Thank you for coming. I hope you had fun despite this."

"I did. Thanks."

Colm led her out to his car. He held the door open for her and then ran around and climbed in while she got settled. He turned the car on and turned to her. "So, where do you live?"

She gave her address and he laughed. "Seriously?"

"Yeah, why?"

"I thought about renting less than a block from you. I went with an apartment in one of the new developments in NoMa since it was a little closer to Kari and Marcus's place."

"Huh."

"In fact, the real estate agent I consulted with even suggested your building as a possibility."

She settled deeper into the seat. "Then I don't need to give you directions?"

"Nope." He grinned and drove her home. Maybe he could get himself invited up for a nightcap.

---

6

*R*adhika watched the streetlights pass as they drove through the city. She was still a little jittery from the scene with Kari's friends. Really, the one friend. The other had seemed shocked at what Tracy said. She jerked when she felt Colm's hand on hers.

"You okay?"

"I will be."

He was silent while they waited for a light to turn green. "That's not a positive answer."

She looked over and studied his profile. His jaw was firm. "It's as positive as I'm willing to get."

"I didn't encourage them." The words were taut.

"I saw you. I know you didn't."

"Even before you arrived. I said hi to them and made small talk, and that was it."

Even to her own ears, her laugh was strangled. She looked back out the window to watch the dome of the Capitol rising between the row houses lining the street. "I'm not asking you for explanations, Colm. What happened happened, and it's on them. They're adults and make their own decisions."

Colm squeezed the hand he still held. She should break his

grip, but the strength wrapping around her was a solid connection she needed more than she wanted to admit. He wove through the streets, and she caught sight of people still walking around. They were crossing the Mall when he turned in between the Capitol Reflecting Pool and the Botanic Garden and parked. She looked at him. "Colm?"

Instead of answering with words, he speared his fingers into her hair and kissed her.

Surprise froze her. Then she moaned and sank into his warmth. Her palm met his chest and stroked. The cotton of his T-shirt did nothing to contain the heat radiating off him. Did his seats recline?

"Radhika?"

"What?" She nibbled at his lips, loving the taste of them. It had been too long.

"Nothing."

He captured her mouth again and pulled her into his embrace as far as her seatbelt allowed. The angle was awkward, but she reached down to feel his tight abs and lower. He growled. As she stroked him, he hardened even further.

Someone tapped on the glass. She broke from the kiss and shielded her eyes from the bright light shining in from the driver's side window.

Colm lowered the window. "Officer?"

Oh, sweet Jesus. Could this get any worse? She sank down into the seat and held her hand up to her face.

"You people realize this is a necking-free zone."

Colm nodded and put his hands on the steering wheel. "We were just heading home."

"Do that."

The officer stepped away from the car, and Colm pulled out of the spot. When they were back on their way, she saw him open his mouth, but she held up a hand to stop him. "No. No. No."

His lips firmed for a moment. "Tell me how you really feel."

"I can't, Colm. Not only because we're coworkers and there's a company policy against this, but I promised myself no more news guys. Not one of you can be trusted to not put your career before a relationship."

He reached up and rubbed the back of his neck, but didn't say anything for the rest of the drive. He pulled up to the drive of her building. "Want me to walk you to your door?"

Radhika thought about it. With Rory and Cecilia home, it wasn't like anything could happen. But she needed a break from him. He was too dangerous with being a nice guy and a phenomenal kisser. "No, I'm good. Thank you for driving me home."

He sat there with his wrists resting on the steering wheel. She wasn't sure if she was glad or not that he made no attempt to touch her again. "Radhika..."

For a moment, she thought he was going to say sorry about what happened. "Don't bother, Colm."

"Bother with what?"

"Whatever you're going to say."

His lips tightened for a moment. "All I was going to say was thank you for coming to the barbecue. I had a great time, and I hope you did, too, despite the ending."

She sighed. "I did. Thank you." She opened her door. "I'll see you around the office."

The muscles in his forearms rippled under his skin as he gripped the wheel again. "Sure. Later."

The building tension didn't dissipate as she watched him drive away. Finally, she stepped inside and waved at the night guard. The condo was suspiciously quiet when she opened the door. Dumping her stuff on the couch, she took the wine into the kitchen to put it away. On the door of the fridge, she found a sticky note from Rory saying that he was using one of the car share services to take Cecilia home and not to wait up.

She let out another sigh. Even better that she hadn't invited Colm up. Without the protection of her brother's sheer presence in the next room, who knows what she would have done.

Her nerves still twitching from earlier, she uncorked a bottle of merlot and poured half a glass. She rested her hips against the counter as she sipped. Memories of her weekend with Colm began to crowd her mind. She'd had the odd couple of hookups since then, but none of those guys had turned into a more serious relationship. Colm had been her palate cleanser after the fiasco with Vince, but she should have known she'd need one to clear Colm from her mind. The mere thought of his lips on hers once again had her nipples tightening.

"Fuck this."

She had the apartment to herself and the opportunity to take the edge off. She was a healthy, thirty-something woman who was in charge of her own pleasure. After pouring another serving of wine, she headed to her bedroom and closed the door. She set the wine on her nightstand and stripped out of her clothes.

Dialing up one of her favorite albums on her phone, she connected it to the external speaker she kept in her room. Candles. She should have candles. She dug her lighter out of the vanity in the bathroom and carried the candles she had there into her bedroom.

Soft light filled the room, a perfect accompaniment to the sensual music. She fluffed her pillows before climbing onto the bed. Closing her eyes, she conjured up an image of Colm from their first night together. He wore the network-issued gear and his cheeks and nose were bright red after being out in the blizzard. There was a light in his eyes that was infectious.

That light told her he'd had fun in the severe weather, but was planning on having even more fun with her.

It was her downfall. She'd never been able to resist the idea of being with a man who she could have fun with in and out of bed. Watching her parents together while growing up had cemented the importance of being with a man who could make you laugh.

They'd taken their time stripping out of their clothes, interspersing the removal of each layer with kisses and groping. She didn't remember any of the words they'd said to each other, but was sure something had to have been said.

Her fingers traced the path his had taken when she was finally down to her bare skin.

She remembered seeing his lips form a word, but before she could ask what he'd said, his lips were on hers. A sigh fell from her lips as she licked them, still tasting him there.

She'd run her hands through his hair. Short and silky, she'd wished it had been a bit longer so she could really dig her fingers in. As it was, he groaned as she massaged his scalp.

His chest hair was rougher than the hair on his head, but still softer than most of the men she'd been with. So pettable. She could have spent hours just stroking him.

The building sexual heat finally stole their patience. She ripped his shorts as she tore them down his thighs. He tossed her onto the hotel bed, his mouth aiming for her pussy.

Her eyelids fluttered as she remembered the feel of his lips on her most intimate place. Heat, wetness, pressure, and suction, all combined to give her one of the fastest and strongest orgasms she'd had in years.

Her legs shifted on the bed as she stroked herself with the memory.

They'd both paused as he climbed up her body, her hand against his shoulder and his forehead on her breast. He kissed the nipple before breaking away.

"Condom."

"Yes."

He returned in what felt like minutes, but probably was only seconds. She welcomed him into her embrace, and he fitted his hard cock against her entrance. He eased in, her inner muscles still quivering in the aftermath. Once he was fully inside her, she let out a quiet moan. The feeling of him filling her was glorious. She wrapped her arms and legs around him, needing him even closer.

He bit down on her shoulder, and the sharp bite of pain caused her to clench down on him.

It was a blur of pleasure from there.

By the time he climaxed, another orgasm began cresting

within her. He reached down between them and massaged her clit until she fell over.

Her body reacted to the memories and her entire body spasmed.

Panting, she finally opened her eyes to the candlelit room.

"Damn him."

7

*M*onday morning, Radhika fired up her computer. She'd spent the remainder of her weekend off-kilter from what had happened on Saturday. But she was determined to start this week bright-eyed and professional. No way would she be caught making mushy eyes at Colm.

She was an adult, goddamn it.

Lee stopped by and thanked her for the work on the scholarship story. They'd gotten a number of phone calls about it and were considering a follow-up story. "Let me know what you need."

"Thanks, Radhika."

"Radhika!"

They both cringed and Lee hunched his shoulders. "Sorry. She's seen me, so she definitely knows you're here."

Radhika took a quick sip from the coffee cup she'd set down when she came in. "Better to get it over with than let her stew about whatever's bothering her."

"Call me if you need me."

"Thanks."

Lee headed out before Bella could get her hands or whatever on him. Radhika stood up and straightened her shirt and slacks. "Morning, Bella. What can I help you with?"

Her boss stopped a cubicle away and narrowed her eyes. "Why didn't you answer when I called earlier?"

Radhika bit back her initial response and smiled. "I just got in."

"You're late."

"No. I'm not scheduled to be in for another hour. I came in early because I wanted to get a head start on some things this morning." Really, she'd been unable to sleep in, but if she'd known Bella was on the warpath, she might have considered calling in sick and binging on some streaming shows.

"Whatever. Come with me." Bella stalked back to her office and Radhika followed.

The few other people who were in the office that early gave her sympathetic looks, but made sure they were busy with other things. She followed Bella into her office and went to sit down.

"Close the door."

"Okay." She did so and sat down.

Bella had her fingers interlocked on the desk and a fierce frown on her face. "I need to know if you went behind my back on this. I do not tolerate disloyalty."

Radhika sat back. "Behind your back on what?"

"I've just been informed that you are being placed on a special assignment with Colm Jones for the foreseeable future and that you're to report to his office immediately. I should have been consulted on this. I should have been offered the position first."

"Excuse me?"

Bella leaned in and hissed. "You heard me. I don't know what you're doing with him to get these special favors, but whatever it is, I will find out. That job should be mine."

What was going on was that her boss was a conspiracy theory nutcase. If this news about a special assignment was real, thank you, sweet baby Jesus. "I, truly, have no clue what you're talking about."

Bella stared at her and Radhika was put in mind of a cobra. She sat as still as she could so as not to provoke Bella. God knew they were both deadly. "Go report to him, but know that I'm filing a complaint. You won't be there long. If I have my way, you'll be packing up your desk and on the street by the end of the day."

"Sure. Fine. May I go?"

Bella sat back in her chair and tapped some keys on her computer. "Yes. Close the door behind you."

Radhika waited until she heard the lock click before she shuddered. Bella's assistant came over when she saw her. "You okay?"

"Yeah, I will be. Apparently, I'm not going to be around for a while."

The woman gasped and held a hand up to her mouth before rushing over and hugging Radhika. "Oh, no. What did she do?"

"Nothing. She told me there's some on-high directive and I'm being reassigned to a special assignment."

"Oh, thank God. You call me if you need anything. You hear?"

"Yes. Thanks."

She patted Radhika's shoulder and let her go. Radhika hurried over to her desk and grabbed her coffee and purse. Bella was filing a complaint? Good luck. She was, too.

As soon as she confirmed with Colm that this assignment was real. She hadn't paid attention to where his office was, so she called down to the operator and asked. When she heard the location, she whistled. She wondered if they would set her up near him. If so, she'd smack a kiss on his lips in thanks. Kissing those strong lips... She shook her head and reminded herself of the no-mushy-eyes promise.

She went up to the floor where all the top national reporters out of the DC bureau had offices and knocked on the closed door. Only a few seconds later, Colm opened it with the phone up to his ear. He held up one finger and opened the door wider for her.

Radhika motioned that she could wait outside, but he shook his head and waved his hand for her to come in. She closed the door behind her and tried to ignore the shiver of awareness that spread through her system. They were alone together behind a closed door for the first time in over a year. She should never have let herself go tripping down memory lane after he left on Saturday.

"I understand, but I feel the senator would have a lot to add to the conversation as she was the one on record who co-authored the last bill." Colm rolled his eyes, but went behind his desk and sat down. She sat down in one of the visitor chairs that he had lining the wall. He pointed at one of the two sitting on the other side of his desk. She shook her head, and he stared hard at her. She mouthed the word "no" at him. He mouthed back "fine."

There was another five minutes of wrangling with the staffer, but it sounded like Colm was able to get on the senator's schedule later in the week. He finally set his phone down and leaned back in his chair.

"Hi."

"Hi."

"Are you up here to find out about the fallout from the party?"

She blinked. "No."

"So, you're not interested in how my sister called Tracy on Sunday and verbally dropkicked her all the way to the Eastern Shore?"

"Whoa."

"Yeah. Apparently, Kari wasn't kidding that this was something that had been brewing. I'm not sure what's going to happen with her other friends, but she's done with Tracy."

"I'm sorry. It's never easy to end a relationship, especially with one of your best girlfriends."

"Yeah." Colm rubbed his jaw. "If you're not up here for that, what's up?"

"I wanted to confirm the news Bella told me this morning."

Colm sat forward, arms on the desk. "She's already told you? I wanted to meet with her beforehand to work out some logistics."

Radhika grimaced. "Well, she is not happy, and said she was going to file a complaint. She thinks the job should be hers."

Colm rose out of his chair. "What the fuck?"

Radhika raised her hands. "Whoa. That's what she said. I wanted to confirm the position offer was real before I headed down to HR myself. Considering the way she talked to me and threatened me, this camel's back is broken."

"What did she say to you?"

The lower half of his face had gotten bright red and he honestly looked like he was a heartbeat away from a heart attack. "Nothing you should worry about. I'm as done with her as I can be. I'll talk with HR about moving my desk to a neutral location."

"Dammit. I don't want you anywhere near her fire."

"I won't be. Like Tracy, this has been in the works for a long-time."

Colm grunted. "Can I at least escort you down to HR? I've got a few words to have with them as well."

Radhika blew out a breath. "It's your time."

Colm grabbed his suit coat from the hanger on the back of the door and escorted her out. The trip down to HR was accomplished in near-silence, with them only saying hello to the few people they passed in the hall. Radhika knocked on the door of the HR rep she'd dealt with in the past. When the man looked up from his computer and saw her standing there, his face fell. "Shit."

Radhika nodded. "Yep. And this time I'm filing a formal complaint."

He sighed and clicked some keys and with his mouse. "Let's get this rolling."

An hour later, fifteen minutes of which were spent by Colm in a private meeting with the rep, they were heading back up to his office. "I am so sorry about this."

Radhika grimaced. "We seem to be saying sorry a lot for things we're not responsible for."

"You're right, but it's still the right thing to do. In this case, it was something I was inadvertently responsible for."

"What did you talk to the rep about?"

Colm opened his office door for her and waited for her to

step inside before he closed it behind him. "I told him about her hitting on me in the cafeteria. She's smart, doesn't put anything in writing, and doesn't say egregious things in front of others. But, from everything I've heard, there's enough people reporting issues to show it's a clear pattern of behavior. I figured I might as well add my voice to theirs. We can't knowingly harbor someone that toxic."

Radhika blew out a breath. "I don't want to think about this right now."

"That's fine. Let's talk about this project."

She reached down and pulled her notebook out of her purse. "What is the project? You're a weather guy."

"Have you heard of the Augustine-Nieto Bill?"

Radhika thought it over. She recognized the names, but not what the bill might be about. "House of Representatives, right?"

"Yes. It's a bill to address climate change, and it's pretty comprehensive. There's a fair amount of fighting about what it covers and what it doesn't. I want to do a series of stories not only about this bill and the role of lobbyists, on both sides of the argument, but also the history of legislation related to climate change and environmental concerns and how they affect the potential passage of this bill."

"Whoa. That's big."

"Yes. It's another reason why I decided the move to DC would be best. This way I'm in the backyard of Congress and can get on their schedules a little easier when they're actually in town."

"Good luck with that."

"For some of the ones I want to talk to, there's a fair amount of sites I need to explore in their districts and states, which may result in local meetings. How available for travel are you?"

Radhika looked up from her notes. "What?"

"Travel? I may need you to do some site visits with me and on your own with a camera crew."

Nights with him in a hotel briefly sped through her mind, but she pushed them right back out. He was no longer someone who happened to have the same employer, but now he was in essence her boss.

"Colm, wait. Why did you really request me to be on this project?"

He met her gaze steadily. "I'm not going to lie. I would very much like to explore a relationship with you outside of the office, but I also recognize this may not be the best time for that. I originally toyed with the idea of asking you to work with me to further us getting to know each other, but the more I researched, the more I learned about your reputation. You are one of the best producers here and you deserve a shot at moving up to the big leagues. If you want it. Off the record, I was also asked to help with your situation with Bella, if I could. I could, and as we both know, it's best that you're no longer working for her."

"So, are you trying to white knight for me?"

"What?"

"White knight. Come in on your charger and save the damsel in distress?"

"No. If I was, I screwed that up since she was an even bigger bitch to you because of me. Flat out, the reason I was even able to get you is because Dean recognizes your talent and agreed that you could be assigned to this project without requiring supervisory approval."

Radhika blinked. Dean? Dean approved this assignment? He recognized her talent? He even knew who the fuck she was? Shit.

"As you heard earlier, I've got an appointment later this week with Senator Isaacs. This is only a background interview, laying the groundwork for an on-camera one. I'll email you a list of other senators and representatives, past and present, that I'd like to speak with. You've got access to my calendar, so schedule who you can. Anyone who pushes back or refuses outright to deal with you, send them back to me and I'll see what I can do.

"I'll call down to IT and authorize you to get a laptop and cell so you can work from home or wherever until we can sort out your office situation. I don't want you going back by Bella. When possible, I want to meet you for lunch so we can touch base and figure out a game plan for what's next. I'll email you the research I've done so far and how I envision the shape of the story. Bring your notes to lunch tomorrow."

She felt like she'd been attacked by a tsunami with all the information he was throwing at her. She had already been composing a text to send to Stacey, Jorie, and Hilda, but this called for drinks immediately.

"Any questions?"

She snapped back to attention. "Not at the moment."

"It's a lot, isn't it? I know you can handle it."

His expression was so kind, she felt that if she pointed out how that could be construed as patronizing, it would be like kicking a puppy. "I know I can, too. Do you need anything from me right now?"

"No. I'll call down to IT, so you can grab what you need from your desk for the next few days and then head down there. I'll also touch base with the broadcast office to let them know you're unavailable. We can sort out your schedule with them later."

"Thanks."

As she left the office, he was placing the first call. "Radhika?"

She turned and looked at him. "Yes?"

"Thanks for joining the team. This story means a lot to me and I know you'll help make it the best."

She nodded and closed the door behind her.

This was the most fucking surreal day ever.

HR must have gotten to Bella as her work area was silent. A few of her coworkers glanced at her as she passed and they gave her a thumbs-up. Unsure of how to take that, she went straight for her cube and gathered her belongings.

As far as she could tell, this was her assigned space until she heard otherwise, so she'd leave most of it, but she grabbed the most precious items in case Bella decided to take her retaliatory tactics to the next level.

Her next stop was the IT offices. While she waited for Colm's orders to be processed, she texted the girls to see if they were available for drinks ASAP. As expected, Stacey and Jorie replied that they could do lunch or later. Hilda was tied up with a client all day, so she wouldn't be available until dinner time. She told Jorie and Stacey to meet her at one of their favorite downtown spots that had fabulous cocktails, and let Hilda know that she'd call her later to catch her up.

The woman who was responsible for the telework equipment came over and had her sign agreements for the equipment and then gave her the laptop and phone and their cords. "This is assigned to you for the next six months or until Mr. Jones rescinds his orders. If you're going to need them longer than six months, you'll need to have Mr. Jones, or your supervisor at the time, send down another order."

"Thanks. Do you have a bag for the laptop?"

"Sure. Give me a moment."

Radhika checked the number of her new phone and pulled out her personal one to input the number as a contact. The woman brought back a bulky black bag and handed it over. Radhika stuffed the laptop and cords into the bag and slung it over her shoulder along with her purse. If the trains were running with no delays, she should have just enough time to get to where they were meeting for lunch.

Of course, as soon as she got down into the station, there was an announcement of a medical emergency at the next stop and all trains were remaining where they were for the moment. She raced back out and managed to flag down a taxi almost immediately. She gave the directions to the restaurant, figuring her sanity was well worth the cost of the taxi.

When she got there, Stacey was standing at the host's podium. She had her phone out with her thumbs flying across the screen.

"Hey, Stace."

Stacey looked up and grinned. "There you are." She gave Radhika a quick hug, then went back to texting. "Jorie got trapped on a client call and is going to be a little late. She says at most another five minutes for the call, then ten to get over here, and don't complain about the fact that she's still wearing her workout clothes. But that she hasn't been to the gym yet."

"Ouch."

"Yeah. Y'all are having days."

"To say the least."

Stacey flicked the strap of the laptop bag. "What's this? You have better taste than a plain black polyester bag. Even if it's for computer equipment."

"Thanks. I need to stop by the store on the way home. Retail therapy of the highest order."

"Want me to come with you?"

"That would be great. I don't know if liquor is going to make a dent in this day."

"Whoa. Midday drinking? I could say something about Mondays."

"I really wish you wouldn't."

Stacey grinned. "But I live to quote lines from plays and movies at you guys."

"And the only ones that we recognize are the ones from movies."

"Philistines, all of you. Except Erin."

"Only because she also works in theater."

The hostess came over. "How many?"

"Three." She looked at Stacey. "Unless Hilda said she could make it and I missed it?"

"No. She's still in her meeting."

Radhika turned back to the hostess. "Three."

They got seated and Stacey unrolled her napkin to place it on her lap. "All right, tell Aunt Stacey all about your horrible, no good day."

*H*alf an hour later, Jorie had arrived and Radhika was two drinks into her lunch.

"She called you a what?"

"She never said any specific names, but implied that I was being disloyal and using sexual wiles."

"That woman needs therapy for something."

Radhika clinked glasses with Jorie. "She said she was going to file a complaint about me being assigned to this project. Since I wasn't the one who did anything about it, I'm not sure who she's filing the complaint against."

"Who would have had something to do with it? Besides Colm?"

Radhika stared at the little bit of cocktail remaining in her glass. "I think our bureau chief."

Stacey propped her chin on her hand. "Whoa. That's big."

"Yeah. Colm told me Dean knew about me and was the one who agreed to the assignment. I didn't even know he knew I existed. I'm not sure if that's a good thing either."

Jorie patted her shoulder. "Well, in this case, it seems like it's a good thing. You think Bella's going to actually file a complaint?"

"Probably. She really is that clueless. I don't know if she realizes how high up this goes. If she does, I'm not sure she cares. I've heard her talk about ruling the office one day. She may be gunning to get Dean ousted. Good luck to her with that. He's a hell of a lot more respected than she is."

"What about Colm? Since he seems to be one of the network's golden boys right now. How much pull does he have?"

"No clue. But when I was down in HR reporting what happened with her, he informed them of an incident he'd had with her as well."

Jorie scowled. "Already? He's only been there a week."

"I know! He told me that after Stacey and I saw them in the cafeteria, Bella made a pass at him. She already had it out for me, so if she heard the story about him asking if I was single..."

"What? When did that happen?"

"His first day. We were alone in the elevator and when the doors opened, the biggest office gossips were standing on the other side, and, of course, those were the only words they heard."

Jorie rubbed her shoulder. "You've had a hell of a week."

"And then some. Anyway, because of what happened with Bella this morning, Colm wants me working away from the office until they get a new space for me set up or Bella is moved."

"What is this story you're working on?"

"It's a project on climate change legislation. I've got a lot of research to read through today. Colm and I are having lunch tomorrow to go over my notes and discuss things."

"This is so romantic."

Radhika and Jorie turned to Stacey. "Excuse me?"

"You and Colm working together. Doing lunch, maybe staying late into the night as the offices around you go dark. And you already know he's dynamite in bed."

Radhika held up a hand. "Stop it right there. He's my boss now. That was already off the table, but it's in another state right now."

"But you guys have a prior relationship. You can bend the rules. What's that term? Grandmothered in?"

"Grandfathered. And a one-night stand does not exempt you from sleeping with your boss."

Jorie rubbed her chin. "But is he really your boss? This is only a special assignment, and you've never answered directly to the reporters for your performance evaluation, right?"

"You, too?"

Jorie shrugged her shoulders. "He's hot, you've already slept together, you'll be working closely and getting to know each other. Why not? Besides, you've met his family. Which you haven't told us about either, by the way."

Radhika slumped in her chair and covered her face with her hands as she felt her resolve wavering once again. "Neither of you are helping. Remember, sleeping with coworkers is a bad thing."

Stacey stirred her straw in her drink. "Well, in Vince's case, it obviously was. I've met some of your coworkers and they're always nice to me."

"Because they're not your coworkers and you wouldn't have to work with them after you slept with them."

"They're still nice."

Radhika blew out a breath. This was getting her nowhere. The moment their waiter stopped by, she ordered another cocktail. If she was going to hell, she may as well go well-greased. One of the other servers brought out their food and she dug into her blue cheese and bacon burger. Today was not a day to be good and stick with her mostly-vegetarian diet.

As Jorie chewed on her burger, she stared off into space. Radhika swallowed her own bite. "Did your client call go okay?"

"Yeah. Do you want me to do something about Bella for you?"

"What? No. Please, do not do anything about Bella."

"The offer's there if you need it."

"I don't want to worry about you getting arrested for identity theft or something on top of this."

Jorie lifted a shoulder. "Like they'd be able to figure out it was me."

"Leave this to HR. I think with Colm filing his report, there's enough of a record for them to do something. Maybe not fire her, but hopefully get her out of the DC office. As far as I can tell, she doesn't have any friends here who'd be willing to go to bat for her. She's managed to burn any bridges she had."

They spent the rest of the lunch talking about how the play had gone for Stacey over the weekend—decent despite the desertion of the leading lady—and plans for Hilda's bachelorette party. The strategy so far was that Erin and Hilda were going to have separate parties, but on the same night, and that they'd meet up at a club later for the two groups to get together and mingle, since there was a decent enough overlap in friend circles. Namely Stacey who'd been the one to introduce them.

"Have we decided who's hosting Hilda's party?"

Stacey and Jorie immediately pointed to her. She narrowed her eyes at them. "Don't think this is going to let you off the hook. How many people are we going to invite? There's only so much space my condo has."

"What about that reception room your building has? Or the roof? That could be fun."

"I can look into the availability of the reception room, but that books up quickly. We might be able to do the roof if it's less than twenty people, but we can't leave anything up there when we go to the club."

Jorie tapped on her phone. "We can build in a half hour or so to clean up and get stuff down to your condo. If I can sleep over that night, I'll help do the rest of the cleanup in the morning."

"Providing you're not trashed."

"You know damn well I'll be up before you, even if I get trashed."

"I do not understand how you get up that early every day."

Jorie set her phone down and picked her burger back up. "Training. Lots of training."

Radhika pointed at Stacey. "You get the list of people Hilda wants to invite. Ask her if we should try for a group rate at a hotel."

"Will do."

Radhika picked at her fries. "I should block out the dates on the calendar with Colm so he doesn't think to send me out on an interview."

Stacey giggled. "You two are so going to sleep together before this is over."

～

Colm rubbed his face as he fought off a yawn. It was already five and he'd been in the office since seven this morning. He should have left long ago, but after the alteration of his timeline thanks to Bella this morning, he'd spent the time he'd planned to use doing more research and calls for background interview appointments on a meeting with Dean, another rep in HR, and one with facilities to get Radhika assigned to an office on his floor. He'd even been called in on the local broadcast to comment on a typhoon that was brewing in the Pacific and taking aim at the Philippines. Thank God he'd been smart enough to bring in his extra shaving kit.

Radhika's office wasn't going to be ready until next week as they had to do some dancing on her getting an office to herself. He pulled some strings with his agent about the clause in his contract about having an assistant assigned to him. It had been HR that had pushed back on it, but after he reminded them of why Radhika was in this situation in the first place and what he was willing to do to make said problem go away, they'd backed down.

It helped that Dean was fully in his corner. Apparently, the Bella problem had been thanks to someone even higher up in the food chain, but that person had left the company and Bella hadn't bothered to make nice with anyone in the DC bureau. HR was researching how to fire her without losing a multi-million-dollar suit. Funny how no one thought a suit could be avoided.

The ringer for his personal cell phone went off, and he dug it out of his pocket. "Hey, Kari. What's up?"

"I know I already apologized to you about what happened

on Saturday, but I wanted to apologize to Radhika in person. Do you have her number?"

"I'll check with her to see if she'll let me share it. Does that work for you?"

"Sure. Thanks."

As soon as he hung up, he pulled up his contacts list and sent her a text asking if he could send Kari her number and explained why.

After working through a few more emails, the chime notifying him of a new text on his personal phone sounded.

R: Sure. But, tell her it's not necessary.

He texted back.

C: Thanks, and will do. How was the rest of your day? You can officially sign off if you need to.

R: You've got a lot of good research. I've made a ton of notes and I'm only halfway through.

C: Don't overwhelm yourself on the first day. I only sent you about two-thirds of my files. The ones you have are the most important, but look for the ones with the double stars at the end of the file names.

R: Already have. Where are we meeting for lunch tomorrow and what time?

C: Consider me a total newbie to town. Where do you suggest?

R: Do you want to stick close to the office?

C: No. And probably not downtown, either. I don't want to risk some staffer overhearing us.

R: Good point. We could go up to Silver Spring, but NOAA's near where I'd suggest...would you be willing to head down to Alexandria? Patents and Trademarks are down there, but we could go farther down King Street. It would be a lot of time away from the office, though.

C: Worth it. It's work-related, so it's not like we're taking off for the afternoon for a date or anything.

R: We'd better not be.

C: The lines are clearly drawn and observed.

R: Good. What time do you want to meet?

C: How about noon down at the King Street station?

R: On the calendar. Speaking of calendars, I've put down the dates for the wedding and bachelorette party. I can't be out of town then.

C: Not a problem. If anything else comes up that needs to be scheduled around, stick it on there.

R: I know I didn't say this earlier, but thank you for this opportunity.

C: Believe me, from everything I've heard, you've earned this.

R: Night. See you tomorrow.

C: Night.

He set his phone down and sighed. Getting Radhika assigned to this project was either the smartest thing he'd ever done, or the dumbest.

$\mathcal{T}$he next morning, Colm cracked his neck as he prepared to get on the Yellow line train to take him across the Potomac. He could have switched over to the Blue line, but when possible, he preferred taking the Yellow across the river so he could see the view of the monuments. It had always been one of his favorite things about visiting DC, especially since he regularly flew in and out of Reagan.

Now that he lived here, he planned on taking advantage of the opportunity every chance he got. The only regret he had about moving here at this time of year was that he'd just missed out on the cherry blossoms and it'd be another year before he could enjoy them.

That got him to thinking about doing a story on weather and weather-related predictions and federal agency resources dedicated to them. The US had seriously fallen behind in weather prediction technology, though it had made some gains after the complete bust of predictions for Hurricane Sandy. Depending on how he did with this series of stories, he might be able to spin off a story or two about funding. He typed a few notes into an app on his phone.

The train came to a stop in front of him, and as expected, it was lightly populated this time of day. He snagged a window seat on the right side of the train and settled in. When they came out of the tunnel to cross the bridge over the Potomac, he put his sunglasses back on. The day had started off with some light showers on their way out to the Bay and gave way to a sunny and cloudless sky. The dome of the Jefferson Memorial rising through patches of trees filled his vision. As they raced across the track, the bright spear of the Washington Monument began to tower over Tommy boy. He counted the Lincoln Memorial, Kennedy Center, and, in the distance, the National Cathedral, in his tally of landmarks.

They were soon back underground and a few soldiers and officers got off and on at the Pentagon. The ones who were clearly traveling together didn't do anything but read newspapers as they sat next to each other. A couple stops later, they rose back out of the tunnel and he resisted the urge to get off at the airport as was his habit.

He watched as residential buildings passed by. The amount of development that had occurred since Kari had first moved here blew his mind. Though he hadn't lived anywhere for long, he'd been in and out of the DC area for over fifteen years thanks to Kari. He wouldn't have thought to call it his hometown, but since he could pick out new developments and list what used to be there—usually an empty lot—with some regularity, it was probably the closest to a hometown as he'd ever get.

They pulled into the King Street station. He scanned the platform, but didn't see Radhika's dark head of hair. He jogged down the escalator and looked around. She was standing outside the gates, gaze focused on her phone. He tapped his card on the sensor to get out and walked over. She didn't look up even though he was standing right behind her, so he cleared his throat. She was frowning as she glanced up, but that quickly turned into a smile. "Hey."

"Hi. Everything okay?"

"Yeah. Just a text from Stacey."

"Must not have been good news since you were frowning."

"Remember we were celebrating the opening of her play on Friday?"

"Yeah. How did it go?"

"I hadn't told you that the female lead in her play ditched them the morning of opening night because she'd gotten a call from Hollywood. The first couple of days were rocky and Stacey was tempted to sic Jorie on the woman."

"To bring her back?"

"No. Anyway, enough critics had been to the preview on Thursday so they got decent reviews and didn't close opening weekend despite the understudy not being as prepared, or sober, as she should have been."

"Ouch."

"Yeah. They managed to pull in another actress who's a friend of Stacey's. It's still not as smooth as it could have been, but she's not only professional, but good, so they're making do. Oh, hey, here's the trolley. We can take that down to the restaurant I was thinking of."

They climbed on and Colm let Radhika lead the way to seats in the back. He waited until they were settled before asking his question. "Are they closing the play early?"

"Probably."

"Is that why you were frowning?"

"Oh, no. It seems Miss Leading Lady and her agent didn't read the Hollywood contract as thoroughly as they should have. The offer was for a one-night guest spot, not a recurring role. She's back in DC and demanding to be put back into the play. Like she hadn't skipped out and breached her own damn contract."

"Is she that dumb?"

"That or way too reliant on an agent who doesn't actually know what he's doing."

"I'm sorry for Stacey."

"Yeah. This is totally for the play's producers and the theater manager to deal with, but the bitch is whining to Stacey because they'd been friendly before this."

"Stacey seems to be friends with everyone."

"Pretty much, but cross her at your own peril. And this idiot firebombed that friendship."

"Good to know."

Radhika glanced up at him. Unfortunately, he couldn't read her face through the dark sunglasses she wore. They covered a good half of her face, but did wonders for her cheekbones. "Normally, because of the lines we have drawn and the fact that I surprisingly trust you with them, I wouldn't mention this. But, Stacey has decided that we are meant to be together. If you find yourself near her, feel free to depress those expectations."

Conflicting thoughts beat at his head with that statement, so he focused on the one that caught him most off-guard. "Surprisingly?"

Radhika rolled her shoulders as she turned her face toward the window across from them. "Yeah. Surprisingly. Let's just say I don't have the best track record with past relationships with fellow journalists. Besides your reputation, the boss/employee thing..."

"For the record, I'm not your official supervisor. I don't think that has been worked out yet, but I won't be writing your performance evaluations."

Radhika lifted her glasses as she stared at him. "We'll get to that in a moment, but you are the person in charge of this special project that I'm assigned to, so whether or not you are my boss of record is splitting hairs. But I've got a rule against dating anyone I work with, especially journalists."

"You slept with me."

"Point A: a one-weekend stand is not dating. Point B: you were a rebound fling and not expected to be seen again. Point C: why aren't you my boss of record and why hasn't it been decided who is?"

"Because of the aforementioned one-weekend stand. I didn't go into details with HR, but I told them we had a past romantic relationship and I didn't want to be responsible for your performance evaluations. Dean put his thumb on the scale to seal the deal."

He couldn't read the expression on her face before she slipped her sunglasses back down. "You are Machiavellian. Remind me not to cross you."

"I'm beginning to think it's you I shouldn't cross."

"I protect myself when needed."

"Smart."

"Female."

"Got it. Where are we getting off?"

"Next stop."

She reached for the signal cord and pulled it. They had to walk another block before she stopped in front of an Irish pub. They advertised a special of fish and chips as well as screenings of soccer and rugby games. "Why here?"

"I like their beer selection and when I've been here during lunches, they've had decently sized tables so we can spread out a bit if we stick to the bar area."

"That'll help."

He'd been distracted on his way out the door so hadn't grabbed his notebook and pen pack. He also hadn't gotten a bag for his laptop yet, but from the way the messenger bag rested on her hip, he'd bet Radhika was carrying hers. "Do you have a pad of paper with you?"

"Sure. I tend to work best with paper, so one of my notebooks is already half-full."

Understanding her silent message that she wasn't sharing, he got back up. "Is there a convenience store around here?"

"Down another block."

"I'll be right back. Order a Guinness for me when the server comes. To the right or left?"

"Right."

"Back in a bit."

He jogged down the cobblestone sidewalk to a chain convenience store and made quick work of his errand. When he returned, a pint glass filled with dark stout sat at the table. Radhika was sipping from a glass of water as she looked at her now-opened laptop.

"How's the Wi-Fi?"

"Decent. Even better is that I was able to log into our VPN."

"Great. Did you order?"

"Just drinks. Pretty much everything on the menu's good, if you're picky."

"I've learned not to be."

The server came over and took their food order. Colm went with the special of fish and chips and Radhika ordered a vegetable boxty. While they waited, Colm opened the pack of pens and scraped one on the notebook paper. It took a few strokes before the ink began flowing. "Tell me what you've learned."

"First, you've got a lot of research to work through. You're going to need to sort out the through line to bring this together into a coherent story. Have you figured out a theme or something yet?"

"Beyond climate change legislation? No. And I know it's going to get worse once we start interviewing people."

"You mentioned that you want to do on site interviews. Do you have an initial list of locations?"

"Some. A fair number of them are near the edges of national parks, so we might want to talk with the park service as well."

Radhika flipped to an empty page in her notebook and began writing down things as he spoke. "Okay. What's your goal for the story? Your audience?"

"I want American citizens to call their legislators and let the legislators know their feelings about climate change."

"Do you want this legislation to pass?"

"Not necessarily. I want legislators to know they can't continue to sweep it under the rug, though."

"Citizen activism?"

"Yes."

"Okay. That's a start. Which of these historical stories speaks the loudest to you?"

They spent the next five hours talking about the story, molding and shaping it. They ordered another round of snacks after they finished their lunch to justify camping out in the pub's bar area. He nursed his Guinness, but ordered another when he finally had only foam left in the first. Radhika stayed with water at first, but then switched over to the harder soft drinks. The battery in her laptop eventually drained down to nothing, so she switched fully over to her notebooks. She hadn't been kidding about needing the other one she'd brought with her, even with the laptop. By the time they finished, he thought she'd filled about a third of the pages in the new notebook.

"I'll start talking to the research department to see what they can come up with on case law with this. I'll also start calling the people on the list you gave me as well as the ones we've come up with today for interviews. For the departments we've identified, I'll see what contacts I can come up with outside of the press office, but I'll also shoot some initial questions through the regular channels. Anything else at this point?"

"I think that's it. Let me check my email to see if anything's come through about your office."

Colm scrolled through the messages and winced. He'd need to get an actual assistant on board to help him sort through and organize all of this as well as make the travel arrangements for him, Radhika, and anyone else they were able to add to the team down the road.

Then Dean's name caught his eye. The subject line did not fill him with joy. "Damn."

"What?"

"Hold on." He read through the email and sighed. "It's from Dean. Bella had a meltdown in the office today and they had to call security. She's in the hospital for a psych evaluation." He looked up and saw that Radhika's mouth was hanging open.

"Seriously?"

"Yeah."

"She's doing it so she's not fired."

"What?"

"I'm not saying that she isn't in need of psychiatric help, but I bet that if they continue the attempt to fire her, she's going to claim that it's discriminatory against her mental health situation."

"You're cynical."

"When it comes to her, you bet your ass I am. It may have taken a while, but I finally learned to trust my instincts about her, and they're all screaming that she did this on purpose and with a specific goal in mind."

"Who wants to get taken to a hospital psych ward involuntarily?"

"Someone who's a hell of a lot craftier than I am."

When the server stopped over, Colm held his hand over the top of his pint glass. "Just the check, please."

Radhika started packing up her laptop and notebooks. "How long is she in for?"

"I don't know. Dean didn't say."

"Probably against HIPAA to discuss that."

"Yeah, it was pretty much bare bones and nothing more than I couldn't have found out when I got to the office in the morning. I'm surprised you haven't gotten an email about it."

She pulled out the office-assigned phone and turned it on. It started a mad series of beeps as soon as it connected to the cell network. She hurried to lower the volume. "Sorry about that."

"Not a problem. You were with me today anyway, and I'd like to think I get priority at the moment."

"Yeah, yeah...oh."

"Message?"

"Yeah. From Lee. Holy shit."

"What?"

"He was there when it happened. She went up to your office and someone told her you were out to meet with me." She frowned.

"Is that problem?"

"Not for me. It's work."

"Exactly. I wasn't expecting any calls, and if anyone really needed me, they could call. But I told one of the other reporter's assistants where I was in case the building got evacuated."

"Well, Bella heard that and that's when she threw her fit. Lee had come up to make an appointment with someone, and he said that Bella started with calling me a whore of Babylon..."

"What?"

"That's what he wrote. She then realized she had an audience and he said it was like watching a lightbulb go off. She started raving about conspiracy theories and how the aliens were out to get her."

"She hasn't talked about conspiracy theories before, has she?"

"From our little conversation yesterday, I would have said the only conspiracy theory she had was I was out to get her for some unknown reason. Otherwise, she was just a shitastic manager."

"I'm glad you weren't in the office for this."

"Me, too. I guess I can go back to the office now."

"I'd rather you didn't." He held up a hand when she opened her mouth. "At the very least, check in with HR."

"It's after hours."

"So call them tomorrow. The plan had been for you to work from home for the rest of the week anyway."

"Fine. There's a coffee shop not too far from the office. I'll camp out there. Bella said the servers were rude to her the first time she was there, so she never went back. I'm pretty sure they told her there were no free refills of latte mochaccinos."

Colm knew it was mean, but he couldn't help laughing. "She is an arrogant person, isn't she?"

"Arrogant, rude, self-absorbed, and believes the world should revolve solely around her. It's a wonder she got as high in the organization as she did."

"Peter Principle."

"I'm sure in part, but that can't explain all of it."

"Some employers have no clue how to read employment histories."

"You've got that right." She lifted her phone. "I need to get back home. I told my brother that I'd make dinner tonight. He's starting college applications."

"Has he decided what to study?"

"No. I think he's doing these as a test run to see how hard they are to work through."

"Couldn't hurt."

"Anyway. What time do you want to meet tomorrow?"

"Text me when you get to the coffee shop. I'll see how my schedule shapes up and I'll let you know by eleven. We can meet at the coffee shop and eat there or head somewhere else if you want something different to eat."

"That works. Are you heading straight home?"

"Yeah."

They spent the trolley ride to the train station and the ride back across the river talking more about the story. Radhika suggested the possible addition of a segment on the environmental impact on and of the Arctic food chain. He mulled that over. Cute baby seals and polar bears would certainly get eyeballs on the segment, but he worried that it might stray a little too far from the storyline. People connected more to what was happening in their backyards, not thousands of miles away.

A lot of the longest lasting legislation that dealt with environmental change was the direct result of the Dust Bowl, but the people who'd been alive then were dying off and the first-person accounts that allowed the emotions of the experiences to impact those who didn't live through it were no longer available.

When they were rolling into the L'Enfant station, Radhika got a weird look on her face. "What's up?"

"I know this is kind of out of left field, but do you want to come over for dinner tonight?"

Colm was surprised by the request, but he didn't want to pass up the opportunity to get to know her better. "Sure. What are you serving? I can bring wine."

"Not necessary. If you want some, I've got a good stock. How are you with Indian food?"

"Love it."

"Good. I'm shooting for serving around seven. That's when Rory gets off work, and his girlfriend Cecilia's coming over, too."

"Shoot me your condo number, and I'll be there."

"Great. Uh. See you then." She rushed out of the closing doors and he watched until she faded from sight.

10

*R*adhika could not believe what she had done. Not only had she screwed up the spices and ruined dinner, but she'd invited Malcolm "Hurricane Hottie" Jones to her home for dinner with her brother and his girlfriend. Maybe if she was lucky there was some brewing natural disaster he'd have to immediately fly out to cover.

She pulled up the weather app on her phone and was disappointed to see clear skies across the country. Not even a lowly rainstorm over the Plains. Wasn't it tornado season? Since she had her phone out, she texted Rory to see if he'd be okay with delivery. His reply was immediate.

Don't care. Hungry. Thanks!

She pulled up the delivery app and ordered their usual from their go-to place for when they didn't feel like cooking for themselves. She thought of Colm and doubled the order of alu gobi, dal, and parathas. A quick check of the fridge showed she had an unopened container of yogurt and a couple of cucumbers. Anything leftover would be fine for Rory's lunch or dinner tomorrow.

There was a knock on the door. Damn it. Was Colm early? She checked the peephole and saw it was Cecilia. She flung open the door. "Oh, thank God."

Cecilia's eyes widened. "What? What happened? Is Rory okay? Your parents?"

"No. No. Everyone's fine. I'm just freaking out here."

Cecilia dumped her work bag, purse, and coat on the couch. "What's going on?" She wrinkled her nose. "And what do I smell?"

"Dinner. In the garbage can."

Cecilia leaned back. "Garbage can?"

"I added the wrong spices and tossed it."

"Well, if you hadn't tossed it, I could have seen if it was salvageable. Remember bingate?"

"Don't remind me. It's in the garbage and dinner is ordered. It should be here by the time Rory's home from work." Radhika headed back into the kitchen. If she was going to survive this evening, she needed wine. She went to the chiller and pulled out one of the bottles she'd gotten on Saturday. "We're having another guest."

"Stacey or Jorie?"

"Why not Hilda or Erin?"

"Because you said one and I've only seen Hilda and Erin here as a couple."

"Well, smarty pants, neither of them. It's a guy…"

Cecilia straight-up squealed. It was like being around Stacey, except Cecilia was more reliably grounded.

"Stop that."

"But you've never brought a guy around since I started dating Rory. And all I hear from him is 'that dickbag Vince.'"

"Do your parents know you have a mouth like that?"

"Not if I can help it. Your brother is a bad influence. So are you, for that matter."

Radhika pulled down two wine glasses. "Thanks, I think. And it's a coworker. We had an afternoon meeting today and, well, I lost my mind and invited him over for dinner when I got off the train."

"Ohhhh. Tell me more. Is he hot?"

"Is he hot? What about is he nice? Friendly? Kind to animals?"

"If he wasn't any of those things, you wouldn't bother inviting him over here when you knew Rory and I'd be here. Answer the question on the table."

"Yes. But he's the head of a special project I've been assigned to, and you remember my rule."

Cecilia raised both hands and made air quotes. "Never again with coworkers."

"Exactly."

"If he's hot and not your boss..."

"Didn't I just say that he's the head of the special project I'm on?"

"You didn't say boss."

"Still out of bounds. And a coworker." She poured half a glass for Cecilia and passed it to her before filling the other glass damn close to the rim.

"Who is he?"

Radhika lifted her glass and mumbled into the wine before sipping.

"What?"

"Colm Jones."

Cecilia squealed again. "Oh. My. God. The Hurricane Hottie! Here! In your condo! Did you know he was in town during the blizzard last year?"

Radhika tried to beat back the blush, but knew she wasn't successful when Cecilia clapped her hand against her mouth. "Oh, my God. You knew. You're blushing. What did you do?"

If Cecilia hadn't become the little sister she'd never had— and she'd beat her own baby brother up if he did anything to hurt Cecilia— she would have ignored the question and gone into her bedroom. Instead, she sat down on one of the breakfast nook stools. "Nothing since the blizzard. We happened to be in the hotel and there was an attraction between us. That was it. It was nearly a year and a half ago."

Cecilia leaned back and sneered. "And you've been mourning Vince after being with Colm? Was he bad in bed?"

"No."

"Then why even think about Vince?"

"I have no clue."

Cecilia came over and hugged her. "Oh, Radhika. I'm sorry."

Radhika patted Cecilia's arm as she tried to lean back. "Why?"

"For whatever drove you to decide Vince was worth a second thought after sleeping with Colm."

Radhika froze for a moment, and then started laughing. She couldn't stop. Even when the tears started coming. Whether it was because she was laughing so hard or something else she didn't want to explore, she couldn't tell. Cecilia, sweetheart that she was, stood there patting her back and periodically handing her paper towels. Radhika finally pulled herself together. "I'm okay. Really."

"You sure?"

"Yeah. I'm going to go wash my face. Rory should be here soon, and so should Colm."

There was another knock on the door. They looked at each other, shock on their faces.

Cecilia was the first to break the silence. "Would he come early?"

"No. He doesn't seem the type." Then she glanced at the clock and smacked her forehead. "Delivery. Let me go pay for it."

It wasn't the food. It was Stacey. Radhika flung the door open once again. "What are you doing here? Aren't you supposed to be at the theater?"

Stacey opened her mouth, and all that came out was a wail. She wrapped her arms around Radhika and cried into her shoulder.

"What? What happened? Stacey?"

Radhika maneuvered with Stacey holding onto her shoulders so she could see Cecilia. "I have no idea what happened. She started crying when I asked if she was supposed to be at the theater."

Stacey let loose another wail.

Radhika frowned and patted Stacey's back. "There, there. I'm sure we can sort out whatever the problem is."

"No, you ca-a-a-a-n't."

Radhika hugged Stacey until she quieted a little. With Cecilia's help, she was able to peel her friend off her shoulder and get her situated on the couch.

Cecilia grabbed the box of tissues that were on the coffee table and held them out to Stacey. Stacey pulled out a handful and blew her nose.

Radhika went back into the kitchen and pulled down another wine glass and filled it halfway. No reason to waste more than that if Stacey spilled it. And hopefully not by waving her arms around in the air. The couch was sitting over the stain from the last incident.

After grabbing her own wineglass, Radhika carried them back into the living room. Cecilia had managed to get Stacey calmed down to a few tears and sniffles. Radhika kicked the ottoman over so it was in front of Stacey. She handed her the second wine glass. "Okay, tell me what happened. And without gestures, if you please. Respect the wine."

Stacey gave her a small smile that wobbled as more tears formed. "They cancelled the show."

"Oh, honey." Radhika leaned over and hugged her. "I am so sorry."

Stacey shrugged her shoulders and took a sip of wine. "It's not like it's a surprise. Though I am totally blaming it on Melissa. She's suing the producers saying she had notified them ahead of time about the Hollywood thing, and it's not her fault."

"The bitch."

"Right? At least the critics saw the preview, so I know it's not my writing that's the problem. Though, they did say the third act lacked punch."

"You can always fix that with the next play. Or go back and improve this one before it gets produced again."

"It probably won't be. It'll always be associated with that bitch."

"Could you go to New York with it?"

Stacey sat back on the couch and slumped down into the cushions. "I don't wanna."

"Excuse me?"

"I said I don't wanna."

"Wanna? What are you? A toddler or a classically trained actress?"

"I'm someone who's had her heart ripped out because a cold as iron bitch who thinks nothing of herself ran off to Hollywood."

"Then blacklist her ass. You're stronger than this, Stace."

"Not right now, I'm not."

"Fine. Want me to call Jorie?"

"No. Do not call Jorie."

"Then what are you going to do?"

"Wallow in your wine tonight."

A muffled snort caught her attention and she turned her head to find Cecilia with her hand covering her mouth and nose as she looked over her shoulder at one of the paintings on the opposite wall. Radhika shook her head and went back to Stacey. "At least that's a plan. Do you want to wash your face? Company's coming."

Stacey sat up. "Who? I'm sorry, I can go."

"No. It's all good. Colm'll be here in a bit."

She squealed and did a little couch dance.

Radhika let her head fall forward and rubbed her eyes. She should have taken Stacey up on her offer to leave if only to avoid having to witness this. She turned and set her glass on the coffee table. Standing, she held one hand out to Stacey who took it. She hauled her friend up and then took the still full glass and set it next to hers. "Cecilia, would you get some glass jewelry so we can tell these apart? We'll be back out in a bit."

"Will do."

Radhika led Stacey back to her bathroom. She grabbed one of her extra washcloths and handed it to Stacey.

As Stacey blotted her face in the mirror, she studied Radhika. "What's going on with you?"

"What do you mean?"

"I mean I'm cleaning tear tracks from my face so I know what I'm seeing on yours."

She waved that away. "These are nothing. I was laughing a little too hard earlier."

"Mm-hmmm. How about we promise not to lie to our friends?"

"It's the truth."

"And I'm betting only a small part of it." She rinsed the cloth, squeezed it, then handed it to Radhika. "If I have to do something to my face to make me presentable, you need to do the same."

Radhika pursed her lips. "Thank you."

"Told ya. Honesty is the best policy."

Radhika swatted at Stacey's shoulder, but she danced out of the way. And right into the toilet. Radhika caught her before she fell. "Careful."

Once she was steadied, Stacey held up her hands. "I know. Most accidents in the home happen in the bathroom. I'm getting out of here. Wash your face."

Radhika stopped her with a hand on her shoulder. "Seriously, are you going to be okay?"

"Yeah. I'm used to disappointments, but this one hurts since it's so completely out my control, and except for one person, it could have been a nice experience. Maybe even spectacular."

"I know. It's not much, but I truly am sorry."

Stacey hugged her hard. "Thank you. Knowing that I could come over here and be welcome was a huge help. The biggest."

"Why not go to Jorie's?"

Stacey grinned. "You're closer." She skipped out of the room.

Radhika shook her head and then looked in the mirror. "Blech." She wiped away the tear tracks.

Once she dried her face, she put on some mascara and eyeshadow. It wasn't until she was lining her lips that she realized what she was doing. "Oh God." The eyeshadow was subtle, and the mascara only emphasized her naturally dark lashes. The lip liner would have to go, though. She only used it with the bright red lipstick she wore when the girls dragged her out to the clubs. She managed to remove most of it, but not all, so she covered what was left with a deep rose lip balm. Not as neutral as she would have liked, but also not advertising KISS ME!

It was bad enough that she'd invited Colm over for dinner. Her heart had been broken enough, and poking at the edges of it told her Colm meant more to her at this point than Vince ever had. She gripped the edge of the vanity and let her head drop.

"Hey, Radhika. The food's here."

She shook herself and hurried out at Stacey's call. Not only was the delivery person there, but so was Rory, kissing Cecilia. She ignored that little display, especially once she realized his hand was inching down to her ass.

Neema, their regular delivery person, handed over three bags of packed up dishes, plates, and utensils. Stacey took them and headed into the kitchen. Radhika signed the receipt and wrote down a hefty tip. "Thanks, Neema. How's the semester going?"

"Good. I'm working on final projects now."

"Good luck, and say hi to your parents."

"Will do. See you, Rory, Cecilia."

They both waved as they continued kissing and Neema giggled as she headed down the hall. Radhika was about to close the door when she heard Neema say breathlessly, "Oh, hi."

Radhika opened the door again and looked down toward the elevators. Yep. Colm had come out with a bag in his hand. And was bent down so Neema could take a selfie with him. He waved goodbye as she got into the elevator.

He spotted Radhika and grinned. "Hey."

She waited until he got to the door. "Any problem with security?"

"Not once I showed them the text from you with your condo number. I hear you're having a party."

"Small one. Select guests only." She had to tamp down the wish it was only a party of two or she'd be all over him the way Rory was with Cecilia.

"I'm glad I'm on the list."

"Come on in." She stepped back so he could. He paused briefly. She looked over her shoulder and saw Rory and Cecilia were still at it. "Break it up, people. Non-family member guests have arrived."

Cecilia wiggled out of Rory's arms, but he tried to resist. Stacey came in and punched his shoulder. "Stop that. As your pseudo older sister, I command this."

That got his attention. "Since when are you my pseudo older sister?"

"Since I met your sister. Stop embarrassing her. Hi, Colm."

"Hi, Stacey. How are you doing?"

"As well as could be expected. I'll take that bag." She held out her hand and he passed the bag over to her.

When Stacey headed back to the kitchen, he bent down until his lips brushed Radhika's ear. Her eyes fell half shut at the sensation of his breath blowing across her skin. "Should I ask?"

Unsure of how her voice would sound, she settled for shaking her head.

"All right." He stood up and held out a hand to Rory. "Hi, I'm Colm Jones."

Cecilia started giggling. Rory looked at her and she tried to stop, but when she couldn't get it under control, she ran into the kitchen. Rory looked between the kitchen and Colm. "Uh, hi. Rory, Radhika's brother. That is—was—is my girlfriend Cecilia. Let me go see if she's okay." He headed back to the kitchen where Stacey's laughter had joined Cecilia's giggles.

Colm looked down at her. "What was that about?"

Radhika sighed and leaned in so Rory couldn't hear their conversation over the one in the kitchen. "Cecilia knows we slept together that weekend. I'm assuming her reaction was due to you arriving and catching her making out with Rory."

"Didn't you tell anyone?"

"Not until I got word you were joining this bureau."

She left it at that and headed to the kitchen to help with the disbursement of the food. Rory was grabbing a bottle of King-fisher out of the fridge. When he turned around and spotted her and Colm in the kitchen, he held the bottle out to Colm. "Want it?"

Colm inspected the label. "Sure, if you've got another one."

Rory grinned. "I keep a stash." He passed over the bottle and dug another one out of the fridge.

Radhika let out a breath as Colm seemed to settle in with her family. Stacey was reaching up in the cabinet where Radhika kept the serving trays. "Don't bother, Stace. We can use the dishes they came in."

"You sure?"

"That I don't want to do more dishes later? Yeah." She and Stacey spread the containers out on the counter and opened them, making sure each had a serving spoon. Once everyone had filled their plate, they headed back into the living room, grabbing a seat where they could.

The conversation was easy and Colm shared stories of some of his more memorable stories, including the one hurricane where he'd shown the wind speed by clutching a lamppost and letting the wind pick his feet up.

Stacey talked about her plans now that the show had closed, and some of the hot plays that were currently in development or production. It turned out that Colm enjoyed going to the theater, so he quizzed her on not only the companies in the area, but the theater sizes and types of productions they usually put on.

Rory and Cecilia had claimed the loveseat, and kept their heads together in quiet discussion unless someone specifically asked either of them a question. After they had mostly cleaned up, Stacey left, and Rory and Cecilia retired to his room, Radhika patted herself on the back for keeping the evening light and interesting.

Colm finished washing the last dish from her earlier attempt at dinner in the sink and set it in the drying rack. "You sure you don't need help with anything else?"

"No, I'm good. Thanks."

"I should be heading home, then. I don't want to keep you from whatever you usually do."

"I have this exacting boss and need to do a lot of reading tonight."

He leaned against the counter, a towel he'd confiscated over his shoulder, with his arms crossed against his chest. "You should tell him to go fuck himself."

Radhika laughed. "Somehow I don't think that would go over well with my last boss in the psych ward."

Colm shook his head. "I still can't believe that happened." He put the towel down on the counter, making sure it was properly folded. "Radhika?"

"Yes?"

He came over and stood before her. Even when they'd spent the weekend together, she'd never felt physically intimidated by him. Now, though, there was something stealing her breath from her.

"Say yes? Please."

She knew what he was asking for. It was the totally wrong decision, but the word she meant to say didn't come out. "Yes."

His eyes didn't leave hers as he bent his head and their lips met.

11

*E*ven as Colm kissed her, he knew it was a bad idea. The worst. But also, one of the best. They had agreed to the boundaries. But her lips were there, gleaming in the kitchen's light. The night together, even with her brother and friends, had been fun and relaxing. Instead of taking the kiss deeper like his body demanded, he broke it.

Colm was marginally satisfied by the hazy look of lust that was in her eyes when she finally opened them. "I'm sorry."

"Hmmmm?"

"Remember, boundaries?"

"Oh, yeah. Boundaries..."

He waited for her to say more, or even kick his ass, but all she did was stand there, looking up at him. What finally brought her back to Earth was a call from one of the bedrooms. Rory came into the kitchen a minute later, holding out a cell phone. "Mum wants to talk with you."

"I definitely should go then. I'll talk with you tomorrow?"

She nodded and put the phone up to her ear.

Rory followed him out. "Nice to meet you. You enjoying DC?"

"So far." He opened the door and Rory held it for him.

"Good to hear. Just so you know, Radhika's the best."

He heard the harder edge in the younger man's voice. "I know."

Rory stared at him for a long minute before nodding. "See you around." And with that he closed the door in Colm's face.

He managed to bite back his laugh until he got in the elevator. Even if her mother hadn't called, tonight was not the night to have the conversation he wanted to have with her.

When he got home, he checked his emails and found a response from one legislator's staffer and another agreeing to a site visit in Colorado. He checked the clock and realized it was later than he'd thought. After setting a timer so he'd remember to go to bed at a somewhat reasonable time, he dug into the emails.

~

The next morning, he was sitting in a meeting with HR. Radhika had been right on the money with her assessment of Bella. They were afraid this hospitalization would make it impossible for her to be fired. He looked hard at the rep. "What about Radhika?"

"Well, there are no current openings she's qualified for. Also, Bella has lodged an unfair hiring practice complaint stating that she should have been considered for the position as she has higher seniority."

"What?" He could not believe he heard those words.

"Unfortunately, she is correct, and we need to provide her the opportunity to interview for the position once she returns."

"No."

"You can't refuse. She has the right to demonstrate her talents."

"Did you not hear me the other day? She hit on me. I'm not going to work with a person who can't respect professional boundaries."

The rep sighed and leaned back in his seat, his pen tapping against the edge of his desk. "Dean has already signed off on this. Unless Radhika can demonstrate superior competency,

Bella has every right to sue." He shrugged. "Just interview Bella when she gets back. Dean said you should call him after we're done."

"This is bullshit."

The rep lifted his hands. "I'm sorry. There's nothing I can do right now."

Not accepting that answer as the final declaration, he headed back up to Dean's office. Forget calling. Better to hash this out in person. Dean's assistant said he was booked in meetings for the next three hours, but he could squeeze Colm in for five minutes before the lunch break. "Perfect. That's all I need."

By the time he got back to his desk, Radhika had texted him that she was at the coffee shop. He replied that he had a meeting with Dean right before lunch, but would text her when he was done and on his way.

When he woke up this morning, he'd thought eliminating the whiff of a boss-employee relationship between him and Radhika would be the hardest task to accomplish today. After that kiss last night, he needed to get at least one barrier to them having a relationship outside of work out of the way. There was no way he would be able to resist pushing against those boundaries for as much as she was willing to give. He had the proposal that had begun brewing in his head as he fell asleep last night ready to go when the HR rep had blindsided him with the news about Bella.

He got up to Dean's office a full ten minutes before his appointment time. The assistant said Dean was still in the meeting and Colm assured him he'd wait as long as necessary. The meeting ran over, but Colm was still able to get his five minutes with Dean as he ate his lunch at his desk.

"What's this?"

"Two things. One, why the hell do I have to give Bella a shot at Radhika's job? You've already approved it." He pulled the sheet of paper from his suit pocket and set it on Dean's desk. "Two, a reorganization proposal."

Dean's brows rose. "What?"

"Answer the first question."

Taking his time answering, Dean chewed on the soup noodles he was having for lunch. "Bella is threatening to sue if she isn't given the job."

"If she's given the job, I quit. I'm within the probation period."

Dean stared at him, and Colm felt the same way he did when his dad had called him on the carpet for his grades back in high school. After a good minute, Dean pushed his soup bowl to the side. "Per company policy, we're only required to provide her with an interview. I strongly suggest you take the following statement under advisement. Have both of them give presentations on what they'd do to develop the story. I'll bring in one of the other executives and the three of us will judge them."

"Radhika and I have already begun working together on this. Making her compete for something she already has isn't fair to her."

Dean shrugged. "Send Bella what you've already provided Radhika and offer to meet with her to discuss things. From now until the presentation, limit your work time with Radhika so Bella doesn't come back with a complaint about equitable treatment. We'll schedule the presentations for a week from when Bella returns."

Colm let out a breath. He wasn't pleased, but he recognized the look on Dean's face, and if he pushed back any more, he'd have his ass handed to him. "What about the reorganization?"

Dean scanned the document and grunted. "Hypothetically, if Radhika were to get this job, why?"

"I think Radhika deserves to be at this level, and with these incidents with Bella, her old assignment may not be safe for her."

Dean stared hard at him, and Colm held his gaze letting the other man know he understood exactly what he had said. "And you're fine with her being on-call to other reporters?"

"If it will get me what I want, yes. I'd want it clear that my story series is priority since you'd already approved that, but otherwise, why not? She's talented and it won't be much different than what she was doing under Bella."

"Except now she'll be working on national stories." He looked at Colm again. "And this way, she's essentially your equal in the organization."

"I noticed."

"I bet." Dean let out a breath. "If, and only if, Radhika passes the presentation and gets the job, I'll consider this."

"Thanks. I'm heading out to meet her for a lunch meeting. Can I share this news with her?"

"Yeah." Dean stared hard at him again. "Be careful."

Colm smiled. "I always am, but a little risk makes life interesting."

Dean shook his head. "Get out of here. I've got another meeting."

Colm saluted on the way out and thanked Dean's assistant for getting him the time. He glanced out the window and saw the rain had started earlier than predicted, so he detoured back to his office to grab his parka from his go bag. The spring shower was enough to wet the ground without forming large puddles. He hoped it would last as the region was experiencing a rain deficit for the year. The coffee shop was only a few blocks from the office, but it was far enough that he could feel the wetness on the cuffs of his pants rising over his sock line by the time he walked in.

He spotted Radhika sitting in the back corner, hair pulled back into a ponytail and bright purple headphones on her head as she stared down at her laptop. When he got closer, he saw her fingers flying across the keyboard, but she still didn't look up. He finally had to tap her arm to get her attention.

She startled and whipped her headphones back. "Oh, Colm. Did you text?"

"Yeah."

"Sorry, I've been working on this and missed it." She pulled her headphones completely off and set them down on the table. "Are you hungry?"

"I am, but I'm thinking of somewhere else for lunch."

She glanced out the window and winced. "You sure? I didn't bring an umbrella with me and I only have my fleece."

Damn. He hadn't thought of bringing an umbrella with him either. "I'll call for a car. I need to talk with you about some things." And he didn't want to do it here where he saw at least three others from their office. They needed to avoid adding to the office gossip pool.

"Okay. Where are you thinking?"

"There's this dim sum place I've been to downtown."

"The one on 7th?"

"That's it."

"It's good. I haven't been there in a while."

He pulled out his phone and sent the request through the app for a car. There was one only a couple minutes away. He held her bag open for her as she put her headphones and laptop away. She slung the strap across her body and followed him out the door.

As the rain had gotten heavier in the time he'd been inside, they were lucky they didn't have to wait longer for a car. He gave the driver the name of the restaurant and they sat back for the ride. A good chunk of DC drivers forgot how to drive any time there was precipitation, and, he saw three near accidents in the first four blocks.

By the time they pulled up to the restaurant, he was seriously rethinking the viability of keeping his car here. But he also couldn't discount the possibility of moving on in a few years and needing it wherever he ended up.

The lunch crowd had lightened up a bit, so they were seated after only a few minutes. He checked around and didn't see anyone he knew lurking. Once the server had taken their drink orders, he leaned in. "I've got news from Dean."

Radhika blinked. "What?"

"First, you were right about Bella. However, not only have they suspended any idea of pursuing termination, she's also filed an official complaint that she should have had the opportunity to interview for the job."

Radhika slumped back in her chair. "Seriously?"

"Yes. I spoke with Dean and he strongly suggested that we have both you and Bella do presentations on how you'd develop the story. You'll need to go off the work we've already done as we also can't have her claiming a time inequity."

She rubbed her face with her hands. "When?"

"A week after she returns. I'm assuming Dean will get word to her so that she can't claim she wasn't notified." He reached across and took her hand in his. "I don't like this. I threatened to quit."

She tried to jerk her hand out of his grip, but he held tight. "Why?"

"You were my choice. I had the latitude to pick my producer. I hate being manipulated."

Radhika's lips twisted. "That's the way she works. I started seeing a therapist a few months after I first started. I finally hit a groove and was able to grit my teeth and bear it. It didn't help that my ex had talked enough shit about me behind my back that my reputation wasn't the best and I had a hard time finding a new job after that debacle. I waited until earlier this year thinking enough time had lapsed to start applying again." Her laugh was acid-filled. "This time it was Bella who salted my employment fields. That day you started?"

He squeezed her hand. "Yeah?"

"I found out my latest application was turned down without an interview. I love living in this city, but I was beginning to believe I was going to have to change cities and careers if I wanted to find a job away from Bella."

"Radhika—" He broke off as the server delivered their drinks.

"You guys need a few more minutes?"

Colm looked at Radhika. "You okay with doing the prix fixe?"

"Sure." She looked at the server. "Prix fixe for two."

The server took the order sheet and scribbled in the appropriate box. "Thanks. Your first dish should be out in a little bit."

Radhika lifted her glass and sipped at her soft drink. "So, what happens now?"

He took a sip of his own drink. "Dean was very clear in saying we should limit our time at work together. I still don't think you should be in your old section. I'll follow up with him about temporarily moving you closer to me." He locked gazes with her. "I would very much like to see you outside of work."

Her breath caught, and she slowly released it. "No."

"Radhika, we can't keep dancing around it."

She looked over his shoulder. Probably hoping one of the servers would interrupt them. He was going to have to do some fast talking to convince her. "Radhika. We've got something together, and it hasn't gone away. I'm not going to lie. I've dated other people since we were together." He paused when she whipped her gaze back to him. He leaned in and took a deep breath before continuing. "No guy likes to admit that he's been a fool. There were issues with my last girlfriend, but the most foolish thing I did was not staying in touch with you. I should have called."

"Colm—"

He held up a hand. "I'm sorry for letting what we had fall to the side. I was an idiot. Will you give me another chance?"

She chewed on her lip. "What about work?"

Her fingers were rubbing the edge of the table, so he reached out again to still them. She turned her palm over so now she was the one doing the gripping. He let his thumb brush against the pulse in her wrist and felt the rapid thump. "You're no longer officially working with me, and I'm not the only one who's going to be making the decision on the presentations."

She took a deep breath and on a rush of air as she exhaled, he thought he heard her say "Okay."

"What?"

She closed her eyes and spoke clearly. "Okay. Whatever this is, I'll give it a shot."

With those words, he thought he could conquer whatever disaster Mother Nature threw his way. He grinned at her. "When's our first date?"

She narrowed her eyes, but the server deposited a plate of chicken satay. She picked one up and bit into it with her sharp white teeth. "I've still got access to your calendar?"

"Yep."

"I'll put it on there."

He crooked his finger at her.

Her eyes narrowed even further. "What?"

"Let's seal it with a kiss."

She glanced around the restaurant, but he tugged on her sleeve and leaned over the table. Her breath puffed against his lips as she paused before kissing him. "You're lucky you're so damn cute."

"I like Hurricane Hottie better than Cyclone Cutie."

"You would."

She kissed him and he felt her smile against his.

12

*T*hree days later, they were standing outside of one of Radhika's favorite places in DC. It wasn't quite a hole in the wall museum, but it wasn't as well-known as it could have been mainly due to its location. Colm lifted his sunglasses. "Marjorie Merriweather Post's home?"

She shrugged her shoulders. "I like walking around here. The gardens haven't filled in much at this time of the year compared to summer, but it's still gorgeous."

He took her hand and lifted it to his lips for a quick kiss. "Lead on."

She fought to hide a shiver. Tugging their hands down, she led the way to the entrance. She was curious to see what his reaction would be. She always felt soothed after a visit and had been nervous about sharing one of her special spaces with him. In the visitor's center, Radhika pulled out her card to pay the entrance fee, but Colm beat her to it. "My treat."

"Thank you."

The docents gave them the little badges to wear and Radhika declined the recorded tour. She'd been here enough through the years to know most of the basics. Colm reached out and took her hand as they walked over to the main house. She didn't realize how stiffly she held herself until he squeezed her hand. Letting out a soft laugh, she squeezed back and let herself lean into him a little bit.

He nudged her with his shoulder. "Tell me about this place."

"This was her home with her third husband who was the ambassador to the Soviet Union. She accumulated a lot of Russian art while they were there. One of the stories is that she'd trawl the secondhand and junk shops in Moscow for relics of the imperial period. Russians didn't want much to do with the royal family back then, so she'd get these amazing pieces for pennies on the dollar. She shipped them back home and a good half of the first floor is all Russian art."

"This is amazing that it's tucked back in the woods like this but in the middle of the city."

"Quite a few people can claim that their backyard is a national park around here."

"Would you ever want to live in a place like this?"

She looked around at the trees and open spaces she could see. The view from the back side of the house was even more spectacular as you could see parts of downtown and the monuments. Mulling over the question, she pushed the front door open. "Maybe. I like the condo and knowing I own it. It's what I can afford, and there's a vitality to living so close to downtown."

"But?"

"Sometimes I miss the open spaces we had when I was a kid. I grew up in the suburbs in the Midwest, so everyone had lawns. Here? You're lucky if you can afford anything more than a condo if you've only got one salary."

"You could go into tons of debt."

"If you're not from the Midwest, you can. I have yet to meet anyone who also grew up in the Midwest who doesn't look at the real estate prices here and start choking." She waved a hand around the portrait and painting encrusted hallway. "It's one thing when you've got a lot of land and a gorgeous house like this. You can totally understand why it's valued for millions of dollars. But when you're walking down a street near a Green line stop and the row houses are going for nearly three-quarters of a million, if not close to a million? That's nuts."

"I take it you've looked."

She smiled. He was worming his way under her skin, and this was the least of her secrets. "It's my sick obsession. I can't not look. It's like a train wreck how high the prices have gone since I bought the condo, which I thought was bad enough at the time. Hell, I needed my parents' help to afford it."

"What about going out to Maryland or Virginia?"

"No, thank you. I do not commute any farther than I have to. Besides, I like being close to Nationals Park."

"You're a baseball fan?"

They walked into a room that was filled with remnants of the last years of the Romanovs and other members of the Russian aristocracy. Radhika had always had the feeling that if Mrs. Post had been able to figure out who to bribe to get her hands on the Amber Room, it wouldn't have been lost to history during World War II. "I'm a fan of baseball park food. Luckily Jorie likes going on a regular basis, so when I can, I hang out with her."

"So, Stacey's an actress. What does Jorie do?"

"Jorie works as a freelance translator...mostly. She works from home, so if I find myself off during a day game, we can head over if I give her enough lead time."

"Does she live in DC, too?"

"Yep. Over by Eastern Market. Stacey's up by here in Cleveland Park. Hilda and Erin are the ones who decided to move to the suburbs, but they're in Old Town Alexandria. It makes getting together a little interesting, but we frequently meet up for brunches."

"That sounds like fun."

"Brunches usually are. Especially when bottomless drinks are involved."

Colm put his hand on the small of her back and pointed to a set of crystal glasses with a gold rim and the double eagle crest of the Romanovs etched in it. "I bet it would be even more fun drinking out of those."

Radhika bit back a nervous giggle as his touch had her feeling very inappropriate for being in a public space. "Come on, there's a lot more to go through." They walked through the rest of the main house with Radhika pointing out some of her more favored pieces. They even stopped in the old kitchen which looked like it could be put back into service at a moment's notice.

Colm looked around the room. "All right. I know I'm not a cook."

She glanced up at him. "What do you mean?"

"I mean I'm in no way excited about any of this. It's interesting, but not exciting. You know?"

She nodded. "I understand. Follow me." She led the way out into the gardens. After winding her way down one path, she pointed out the functional sculpture.

Colm bent close and examined the metalwork of the sundial. "Okay, this is getting me excited. But this is from the twentieth century."

"How can you tell?"

He pointed to the thing in the shape of a sailboat. "That. My dad has a thing for sailboats, so I got to know the shapes of the historical styles. Do they have any others?"

"Not that I'm aware of. We'd probably have to check out the Naval Observatory for that kind of thing."

"I'll put that on the list. Is there anything else you wanted to point out to me?"

"You're not entranced by these views?"

He stood and examined their surroundings. "It is spectacular, and I do appreciate you bringing me out here, but I'm kind of in the mood for something else."

She fought back the disappointment she felt at his words. "What are you thinking?"

"Do they rent blankets?"

Her mind went blank. "What?"

"Blankets? So we could do a secluded picnic. I thought I saw a cafe or something in one of the other buildings."

"A picnic?"

"Yeah, I'm getting a bit hungry, and I like the idea of feeding you bits of food as we sit and talk, and maybe snuggle a bit." He waggled his brows. "We could get a bit naughty."

Her earlier thoughts were tame compared to the images racing through her head right now. She shifted on her feet, but the feeling of her thighs rubbing together beneath her dress didn't help matters. "Um, I don't think they do."

"Too bad." He leaned in until his lips were brushing the curve of her ear. "We'll have to remember to bring our own the next time we come back."

"Come back?" Even she could hear how breathy her voice was. Damn him.

"Sure. You like this place a lot, don't you?"

"It's one of my favorite places."

"So we'll come back some other time with a blanket and food."

She shook her head. "You keep throwing me curveballs."

"Show me what else you like about here." He wrapped his arm around her shoulders and she led him back to the paths to the outer buildings and exhibits.

～

Two hours later, they were ensconced in a little basement restaurant just off Dupont Circle. Colm had ordered a flight of bourbon. The bartender had recognized him as they'd both been in Seattle at one point in their mutual pasts.

"What are you doing here, man?"

"Change of scenery."

"I get you. If you're ever stuck here for a hurricane or something, feel free to come here to do your live shots. We'll keep you warm and toasty."

As the guy left laughing at his own joke, Colm shook his head and lifted one of the shot glasses. "Would you like a little?"

She wrinkled her nose. "No thanks. It all tastes like turpentine to me. Breaks my da's heart."

He leaned in close. "Wait a minute. Say that again."

"It breaks my da's heart?"

He sat back and pointed at her. "I knew it. You've got an accent."

"I do not."

"You do. It's really faint, but I can hear it now. I can't quite place it."

She sipped the wine she'd ordered. "Probably because it's no place."

"Where in the Midwest did you grow up?"

"Minnesota."

He nodded. "That's a little bit, but not all of it. Did you ever move around?"

"Nope. Twin Cities, born and raised."

He sipped and hummed as the liquor slid down his throat. "Good stuff." He pulled out his phone and typed something into it before setting it back down on the table. "Okay, what about your parents? Are either them from outside the US?"

"Both of them. Da's from Ireland and Mum's from England, London to be specific."

"Yeah, London seems like its own country sometimes. How did they meet?"

"University. They were both in the engineering program, decided they liked each other, got married, and then both got jobs with the same company they're planning on retiring from in a couple of years."

"Cool. My mom and dad met in elementary school. He was her best friend's older brother, but they didn't get together until he came home for the holidays from his first posting and she was a junior in college. Once she graduated, they got married and she was a stay-at-home mom who traveled all over the world."

"That must have been interesting for her. Seeing the world and all."

"She always said it was the dream job she never had to apply for. She had studied hospitality and had been planning to work in hotels in the hopes she'd be sent to other countries."

He had a smile on his face as he talked about his mom. "You mentioned you'd been to boarding school. That must have been tough on her?"

"A little bit, but she's an adventurer at heart. She's actually got a column in a magazine. She's been writing it for twenty years."

"Really?"

"Yeah, it's a combination advice column and travelogue."

"That's really cool. Do they ever come to visit since you and Kari are here?"

"Kari mentioned she had an email from Mom about coming out in the summer, but I haven't heard anything. Half the time I don't think Mom bothers contacting me because I'm on the road so much."

"I would think she'd encourage one of her kids in enjoying what she does."

"I think it's more the fact that I'm usually doing it on such short notice without extremely detailed plans at least a month in advance that gets to her."

Their food was served and they dug in.

Radhika picked at her sweet potato fries after finishing her veggie burger. "Can you see yourself ever settling down?"

He lifted one shoulder. "Maybe. I haven't given it that much thought honestly. I enjoy my life, and there's a certain amount of flexibility you need to have."

"Okay, so if settling down with the perfect wife to produce the next generation of perfect kids isn't your life's goal, what is?"

"What do you mean?"

"I mean, what drives you in the morning?"

She'd somewhat expected him to give her a glib answer, but instead, he cut a piece off the steak he'd ordered and chewed. The entire time, he kept his gaze on her, but she could tell his focus had turned inward. She sipped her wine, letting the silence stretch.

"There's the work goals, but that's not what you're asking, right?"

"It's probably a little bit. Everyone's got career goals that influence their personal goals. Some more than others."

"I'm not sure I've got any hardcore personal goals. I've enjoyed being the one that gets sent out to cover blizzards, hurricanes, and the like, but I'm also really excited about working on the types of stories that we'll be doing that will hopefully have some even more long-term impacts beyond disasters. I've gone where the job takes me. The decision to move to DC was partly so I can work on the long-term impact stories, and partly so I can spend more time with Kari, Marcus, and Nya. But where I see myself personally in five years?" He shrugged his shoulders and cut another piece of steak.

She appreciated his honesty even if she wasn't sure what to do with it. It wasn't like she was cycling through the dating pool in the hopes of coming up with a winner to walk down the aisle with. Not that the pickings had ever been that deep for someone who wasn't looking to be a political spouse. At the same time, for a man who seemed to be as driven as he was, the fact that he didn't have personal goals surprised her. He hadn't struck her as a complete workaholic.

He sliced another chunk from his steak. "What about you? What's your five-year plan?"

She popped another fry into her mouth. "The last few months I've been focused on getting out from under Bella's thumb. If I do succeed in truly getting the job..." She paused as she imagined having the weight of Bella permanently off her back. She hadn't been able to fully savor it before things had gone sideways. Shaking her head, she picked up another fry. "I'll figure out new goals once that happens."

"If it makes you feel better at all, I think people have had their eye on you for a while."

"What makes you say that?"

"I don't think I would have had as easy a time getting you placed on my project, at least at first, if they hadn't been aware of you already."

"Hmmmmm..."

"You could move up if you wanted to. Maybe even New York."

"I'm not sure that I'd want to. I like living in DC, and I own my condo. That's the thing that's pissed me off most about the situation with Bella."

"You could always sell."

"Easily, but there's some comfort in knowing you have roots. At least, for me there is."

He paused in cutting into his steak. "Does it bother you that I don't have roots?"

"I wouldn't say you don't have roots. You've got your parents and your sister and her family. Your roots kind of grow sideways instead of straight down. So, no, it doesn't bother me that you're not particularly rooted to one place."

"What are your personal goals? Do you want to kick your brother out and move some guy into your condo?"

Radhika snorted. "I'm the one most frequently kicked out these days."

"That doesn't answer my question."

"I'm not exactly sure. If you'd asked me that question before the blizzard, I would have expected a ring on my finger by now."

He blinked and she could have been legally blind and still read the surprise on his face. "Engaged?"

"And probably married."

"What happened?"

"He left me. Hence the rebound fling."

"The bastard."

He sounded so much like Jorie that she laughed. "Looking back, it was more of a surprise than it should have been. He dated me long enough to meet his next conquest."

"Asshole. I hope she kicked him in the balls."

"From what I understand, they're still happily dating. Of course, it helped that I was able to make his stories look so good that he's now a special correspondent for one of the morning shows and lives in New York."

It was fascinating to watch the range of expressions cross his face. When he shouted out Vince's name, she realized he'd been cataloging all the personalities on the major network morning shows.

"You dated and were nearly engaged to Vince Rizzoli?"

"Let me clarify that *I* thought we were considering marriage. Nothing was set in stone. As he was very careful to do. It would be bad for his image to leave behind a number of ditched fiancées. Frankly, I'm betting he doesn't feel like spending money for jewelry on anyone but himself."

The corners of Colm's lips lifted. "I've briefly met him. I would agree."

"It is one hell of a pinky ring."

"I'm pretty sure they had to come up with a special lighting plan to downplay it."

They looked at each other and dissolved into laughing fits. Radhika wiped the tears from her eyes. "We are nasty."

"It's the truth."

She let out a sigh and ate the last of her fries.

"Vince is the reason you came up with the no dating coworkers rule, right?"

"He was definitely the tipping point."

"I can promise you I'm not using you to make my stories look good just so I can move to New York."

"That I believe. You'd be there already if you truly wanted to be."

"Thanks. I think."

"Definitely a compliment."

They sat in silence while Colm finished the rest of his steak. Radhika thought it would be tense after what she'd revealed, but she didn't feel like talking for the sake of talking, and Colm appeared to be happy downing his steak in steady, easy bites.

When they were both done, Colm signaled the bartender. He came over and set the plastic billfold with the check down on the table. "Everything okay?"

"Very good. Thanks."

"Great. Give a shout if you need anything else."

Colm shook the man's hand. "Thanks."

Radhika pulled out her wallet to pay her portion of the bill, but Colm waved her away. "My treat. Thank you."

"I don't want to take advantage of you."

He laughed. "A museum date and lunch is not taking advantage of me." He took her hand and leaned in. "I really enjoyed spending time with you today. When can we do this again?"

His thumb was rubbing the center of her palm, and her

earlier steamy thoughts came rushing back. His thumb was a sexual lethal weapon. When the words came, they were a tad breathless. "How about next Saturday?"

He frowned. "I think I have a PR shoot next weekend."

"I'll look at your schedule and let you know."

"Do that."

Colm signed for the check and they headed back out to the Circle. "How are you getting home?"

"Metro."

"I'll walk you there. Today's so nice, I think I'll walk."

They stopped off to the side of the escalators. Colm tugged on her hand and she looked up at him. His lips were on hers and she sighed. They were as strong as she remembered and as deliciously devious.

When he lifted his head, all she could think of was inviting him back to her place even though she wasn't sure if Rory had mentioned if he and Cecilia were staying there or not.

Colm gave her a little push toward the escalators. "I'll see you Monday."

She nodded and waved. She got on, and turned to watch him. He waved and she waved back. As she descended into the station, she watched until she couldn't see him anymore. His gaze never left hers.

13

Two weeks later, Radhika was rushing around her apartment, tossing magazines and clothes out of the way. She'd promised to meet the girls at the bridal salon, God, ten minutes from now. Metro was out with the game today. Though, that meant there should be a decent amount of taxis trolling the area. But she needed to leave *now*.

"What are you looking for?"

She glanced up at Rory as he walked out of his room, scrubbing his head. "My sapphire earrings from Mum. I thought I left them on the table last night, but they're not here now."

"Have you checked your purse?"

"Of course, I did." Rory stepped back with his hands out. Radhika realized she was spiraling out of control. She paused, closed her eyes, and drew in a deep breath. "I did."

"Take everything out one at a time. I'll go through this while you do that." He gestured at the mess on the dining table that more often than not functioned as her desk.

She slammed her purse down on the breakfast bar and began taking everything out, one item at a time. She got to the bottom and held the purse upside down, shaking it, and heard tinkling as metal met granite.

She grabbed the earrings before they could fall off the counter. "Got them."

"Good. Aren't you supposed to be meeting Hilda and the girls?"

"Hence the frantic search. We're supposed to finalize the dresses today and I needed these."

"Get going then."

She looked up at the microwave clock. Five minutes until she was supposed to be there. "Fuck."

She jammed everything back into her purse, making sure to put the earrings back into the velvet pouch they'd fallen out of and that into the little zippered bag where she kept her cards. Tearing out of the apartment, she yelled goodbye to Rory and headed for the elevators. Thankfully, one came quickly before she could decide taking the stairs down from the tenth floor would be faster.

The taxi situation was even better than expected and she climbed into one almost as soon as she stuck out her hand. She gave the bridal salon's address and started texting the girls that she was on her way.

Stacey texted back a picture of her and Jorie holding filled champagne glasses.

R: Save one for me!

S: How far away are you?

R: In taxi and just left apartment. Had trouble finding my earrings.

S: Did you find them or do we need something stronger than champagne?

R: Got them.

S: See you when you get here.

Once they'd gotten out of her neighborhood, the traffic wasn't too bad and they got to the salon only twenty minutes after she should have been there. She walked in and spotted Stacey and Jorie sitting in lounge chairs. "I'm here. Where's the champagne?"

Jorie stood and went over to a small table with a bottle of champagne sitting in a chiller. She poured a glass and handed it over. "Perfect timing. Hilda decided to try on her dress while we were waiting."

"Is she here?" Hilda's voice floated out from the dressing area.

"She's here and getting liquored up, so make it fast."

Radhika glared at Jorie even as she drank half the glass of champagne. "We're friends again, why?"

Jorie sat back down and picked up her own glass. "You puked on me. We should get you a little charm necklace to commemorate that."

She sneered. "Ew. Where would you even get something like that?"

Stacey held up her phone showcasing a necklace with a charm showing the profile of a face and a glob of something coming out of its mouth. "Etsy."

Radhika slapped at the phone. "You two are nasty."

"If you nasty women are done, how about telling me how pretty I look?"

They turned to face the mirrored area where Hilda now stood. The gown was tea-length with a satin underskirt and bodice. It reflected light in a rippled pattern. A beaded lace robe was belted at her waist, giving her the look of someone from a fashion bridal magazine from the 1950s. All she was missing was a little pillbox hat. Stacey and Radhika sighed while Jorie gave her a thumbs-up.

"You look gorgeous. Erin is going to flip her lid when she sees you in this."

Hilda grinned. "It still needs to be fitted, but it's close."

The salon owner came over and fussed with the dress. "You'll need heels with this. Have you gotten your foundation garments, yet?"

"I'm wearing them."

"Perfect. We can do the fitting now if you'd like."

"That would be great. It gives these three time to get sorted for their fittings."

The owner signaled for one of her saleswomen and then led Hilda back to the area where the seamstress handled the fitting.

The saleswoman came over and smiled at them over her tablet. "Now, I have Marjorie down for the ruby red dress, Radhika for the sapphire blue, and Stacey for the amethyst."

They all nodded and followed her over to the dressing rooms she'd assigned them. Radhika slipped out of her leggings and oversized shirt. While she'd remembered the earrings, she'd blanked on wearing the bra she'd planned on wearing with the dress. They'd just have to compensate.

She pulled on the dress and found out she'd forgotten that it had a boned bodice. She might be able to get away without the bra.

The back was fastened using lacings like a corset, so she held up the bodice and stepped out of the dressing room. Jorie opened the door across from her and looked her up and down. "Damn you."

"What?"

"You're not even wearing a bra, are you?"

"Nope."

Jorie clutched the dress's top closer to her boobs. The bluish-red of the dress reflected gorgeously against Jorie's deep brown skin. "I'm probably going to need a real corset to go under this."

The saleswoman came over. "Here, let me get you laced up. This dress should have enough support built in for double-Ds."

Jorie looked over her shoulder. "I'm triple-D."

The woman eyed her. "You should still be fine. It helps that your torso is slim."

Stacey stepped out of her room, already laced and tied. "All set. Who needs help?"

Radhika scowled at her. "How did you do that?"

"Many years of dressing myself between acts. Turn around."

Radhika did as Stacey instructed and felt the laces tightening up her back. At one point, Stacey pulled so hard that she grunted.

"Now lift your boobs."

She reached in and adjusted herself. There was another tightening of the laces, and then she felt them being tied off. Stacey tapped her shoulder. "All set. Let me see you."

Radhika turned back around in time to see Jorie leaning over and shaking her shoulders. She looked at Stacey. "Should I have done that?"

"Nope." Stacey pulled up the bodice of the dress on one side and then smoothed her hand down the front. "How does that feel?"

"It's a bit tight."

"It should be. You don't want it falling down to your feet in the middle of 'Cotton-Eyed Joe', now do you?"

"I thought Hilda said that was on the banned list."

"We'll see what the DJ's bribe level is. It's not a wedding unless everyone's kicking up their heels, now is it?"

"You bribe the DJ to play that song and I will not be held responsible for what I do to you."

Stacey turned her attention to Jorie with her brows raised. "Empty threats, and I know it."

Jorie's face was as set as Radhika had ever seen it. "Try me."

Hilda called from the mirrored area. "You guys ready?"

"In a second."

Radhika went back into the dressing room and took the earrings out. She put them on as she walked back to the common area. Jorie had slipped on the shoes she was planning on wearing. She really needed to carve out time to order hers. She hated shoe shopping.

The three-inch heels put Jorie a good five inches taller than Radhika in her bare feet. Stacey had also pulled out a pair of kitten-heeled slingback shoes, but they hadn't been dyed yet. Radhika followed them out to the mirrored area. Hilda stood there and clapped her hands. "Oh, you guys. You look fabulous!"

She went over to her purse and pulled out three small boxes. "I know these are early, but I wanted to see you wearing them with your dresses today." She checked the bottom of each box before handing them out.

Radhika opened hers and grinned. She went over and hugged Hilda. "Thank you. This is gorgeous and will go perfectly with the earrings."

"I know. I hope you don't feel bad, but I got Jorie and Stacey earrings to go with their necklaces since I knew you were going to be wearing your mom's. I also had the jeweler try to match them somewhat."

Stacey squealed and jumped up and down before coming over and hugging Hilda. Jorie came over and gave Hilda a short hug.

Hilda waved her hands at her face. "Okay, you guys. Put them on so I can see my brilliance."

They all laughed and did as instructed. She'd had necklaces in the shape of their initials made from gold and gems matching their dresses. Radhika gently removed the gold chain from the box holder and set the box down. She undid the clasp and then put it around her neck. The 'R' settled just above where her dress-induced cleavage started. The four of them stood in front of the mirrors.

Hilda grinned. "We rock. I have the best bridesmaids."

They all high-fived and then Radhika, Jorie, and Stacey took their turns with the seamstress. Once she was done, Radhika headed back to the dressing room to change into her street clothes. Hilda had made reservations for lunch at a nearby restaurant, and they were cutting close to time because of how late she'd been.

She slipped her feet into the flats she was wearing and stopped at the desk where the saleswoman who'd been helping them sat. Radhika handed over her credit card to make the final payment on the dress. The woman opened a drawer and pulled out an envelope. "Here's the fabric sample we had made up if you'd like to have shoes dyed to match. If you choose not to have them dyed, we recommend getting a nude shoe."

"Thanks." She checked the envelope and saw that it had a piece of paper pinned to it detailing the dye information. She slipped it into her purse and then signed the tablet.

Stacey came over and repeated the process.

Once they were all ready, they headed out to the street to walk to the restaurant. Radhika slipped on her sunglasses as the sun peeked out from the clouds. They talked about the dresses and potential shoe ideas for Radhika as they walked the few blocks while dodging the tourists who clustered together in the middle of the sidewalk. Once they were seated at their table, Hilda turned to Stacey.

"Has that class started yet?"

Radhika looked at Stacey. "What class?"

"After the play ended, I got a call to see if I would be a last-minute replacement for one of the improv instructors. She'd warned them that it was a possibility, at least."

"Are you enjoying it?"

When a blush bloomed up Stacey's face, Radhika curiosity was piqued. She glanced at Hilda and Jorie and saw they'd both noticed their friend's unusual reaction. Jorie straightened in her chair. "What's with the blush?"

Stacey met Jorie's gaze head-on without blinking. "Blush? What blush?"

Radhika waved her hand in front of Stacey's face. "The blood that's flooding the little capillaries under the skin of your neck and face. You're bright red. What's going on?"

"You guys are imagining things."

"You're evading."

"Nothing, okay. Nothing is going on."

"Mmhmm." Hilda leaned in closer, but before she could say anything else, the server came over for their drink order.

By the time they'd given it to him, and he'd disappeared, Stacey had gotten the blush under control. Radhika, Hilda, and Jorie shared a look. They weren't going to let this pass completely, but pushing now would only cause Stacey to shut them down completely.

"How long is the class going to run?

"Another eight weeks. It was a ten-week class total."

"How many students do you have?"

"About fifteen. It's been a while since I've taught, and I was late the first day, but it'll be fine."

Radhika studied the menu as she sorted out Stacey's answers. Everything was straightforward, even the mention of being late on her first day, so she wasn't sure what was tripping her friend up about the class. When the server came back with their drinks, he took their food order and left them to talking.

"Radhika, how are things going with Colm?"

She'd taken a sip of her wine, and it took everything in her not to snort it back out. As it was, she had to cough to clear her throat before answering. "Fine. Why do you ask?"

Stacey traced a pattern on the table. "No reason. Since that night we all had dinner, you haven't mentioned him much."

"We've been busy."

Hilda waggled her brows. "Fun busy? Do tell."

Radhika rolled her eyes and circled her finger among them. "Us. I meant all of us were busy. Besides, there hasn't been much to tell." The kisses that he'd ended each of their dates with felt too special to be calling up her friends to deconstruct.

What they were building one small block at a time felt too precious and fragile. As it was, she was the one who'd wanted to take this relationship slowly. If she could have gone back and smacked herself silly for not sleeping with him again the minute he'd expressed interest, she would have.

It didn't help that she'd been busy running around with pulling together the presentation for first segment she wanted to do of the larger climate story, and filling in on regular broadcasts when needed. In fact, she was due in later tonight and all day tomorrow to fill in for one of the producers who'd ended up in the hospital yesterday for emergency surgery.

She'd also been in talks with one of her colleagues from the local broadcast, Anita Lewis, about her contacts on the Hill. Anita was supposed to be meeting with Colm for lunch about that today in fact.

Radhika and her girlfriends hadn't been the only ones busy. Colm had taken a few trips out of town to do interviews and research.

He'd called her from Atlanta the other night and had sounded dead tired. She liked to think she'd gotten to know his moods a bit, because in addition to the tired, he sounded a little sad. When she'd asked what was wrong, though, he'd brushed her off saying it was nothing. Just some news about a former coworker.

Hilda broke into her reminiscence. "How's the presentation developing?"

"Pretty good. I'm focusing on what I'd like to do for the first segment, and if I get chosen, we might be have it ready to air in a month."

"Let me know when it does, and I'll have Erin program it into the DVR."

Radhika saluted with her wine glass. "I appreciate your assumption that I'm going to get the job."

Hilda grinned back at her. "You've got this in the bag."

"I can hope. Colm met with Bella yesterday to go over the research he'd sent to her when she came back. He made sure one of the assistants from his floor was present to take notes on what they discussed. Word got back to me that as soon as Bella spotted the assistant, she buttoned up her shirt."

Stacey leaned forward. "What?"

Radhika shrugged. "I have no clue what's going through her head, but she's obviously trying to make some kind of play for Colm. It's going to piss him off. He told me his last girl-friend did a number on him, but he hasn't said exactly what. I just know he hates it when he thinks someone's trying to use him."

Hilda drummed her fingers against the tabletop. "How close do you think she is to getting fired?"

"I think she's a lot closer than she thinks she is. She'll do whatever she can to drag it out, though."

Jorie rolled her neck. "Let's talk about something more fun. Have you asked him about coming as your date to the wedding?"

Radhika set her wine glass down. "Are we still on this?"

Jorie grinned. "Stacey got to have dinner with him at your place. I think you should do us all the favor of getting to know him. It's not like we have a chance every day to hang out with famous people."

"I'm not bringing him to the wedding just so you can hang out with someone famous."

Hilda raised her hand. "Actually, if you bring him, we might be able to get featured in the wedding recap pages."

"What?"

"Our photographer mentioned it as a possibility the last time we met, and Erin now has it in her head that she wants us featured."

Radhika stared at her friend. "Seriously?"

"Dead serious. Could you at least consider it?"

She let her head fall forward into her hands and rubbed her temples.

"I take it that's a tentative yes?"

Radhika flipped Hilda the bird.

"Uh, excuse me?"

She looked up and saw the server carrying the plates of food. She sat back so he could place hers in front of her. Once they were settled, he asked them, "Need anything else?"

Jorie and Stacey ordered refills for their beer, but other than that, they were set.

The discussion moved on to a client of Hilda's that had been giving her a hard time with ordering fabric samples and then deciding she didn't like any of them and ordering more.

"Can't you charge her after a certain amount?"

"Not really. I can at least have them on display at the office, but this is the fifth round and I haven't got a clue as to what she really wants. Other than spending her husband's money."

"How's he feeling with all of this?"

Hilda shrugged as she speared some of her salad with her fork. "I haven't seen him since our initial meeting where he laid out the budget. I've offered to meet with him, but she continues to blow me off saying he's too busy and it's all in her hands."

Jorie tapped her finger against the table. "What about tacking on a service fee to the final bill?"

"Believe me, I'm thinking about it. It's not something I regularly do, but when they take up so much time I'll do it on a case-by-case basis. What I'm really worried about is that she's going to pull this crap once we've started ordering the furnishings."

"So put it in writing that once you've ordered, there will be an additional fee on top of whatever the manufacturer charges for the return of goods."

"I might. I'll copy the husband as well. If they both sign off on it, then I'll do whatever they want because, hey, free money."

Stacey leaned in. "Hey, isn't that Colm?"

Radhika choked down the bite she'd just taken. "What?"

Stacey pointed to someone behind Radhika. She turned her head. The guy had a similar cut to his blond hair, and was roughly the right shape, but he didn't have the right tone of tan Colm had gotten from his visit to the South. She shook her head. "It's not him. He's meeting with Anita Lewis for lunch in the District."

"Why?"

"If I get the job, I want to bring her in to help develop some of the story. She's still got great contacts on the Hill."

Hilda grinned. "Maybe we should get Radhika to invite all of her coworkers. Enough of them work on-air that they're at least locally famous."

Radhika balled up her napkin and threw it at Hilda. "No."

"You are way too much fun to torment."

$\mathcal{C}$olm sat back in his chair and rubbed his neck. "Anita, I don't know what to tell you. With the issue of Bella, I haven't decided exactly how to expand the team yet."

Anita Lewis, one of the anchors for the local news broadcast sat back in her chair and stirred the cocktail she'd ordered. They'd ordered a few of the appetizers to share and were enjoying the outdoor seating a block away from the congestion of Connecticut Avenue.

"I can bring a lot to the table. I've made contacts with staffers here, and you have to admit, that's an area where you not being a local won't exactly help you."

She was right. He'd had a bit more success reaching out to the home office staff, but even they weren't the friendliest when the legislator wasn't inclined to discuss their stances against climate change legislation. There was one who was calling *him*, but as the man's boss was a media hound and chased every reporter no matter the topic, Colm had stuck him low on the list of people he wanted to talk with since his record on climate and environmental issues was virtually nonexistent.

Anita sat forward in her chair, an intense look on her face. He appreciated the woman's drive, but right now all he could think of was the possibility of when he and Radhika could next have time together on their own. His travel and her work schedule had limited the dates they'd been able to go on the last couple of weeks.

He'd hoped to be out on another date with her today, but she had plans with her friends for something for the upcoming wedding. Anita reached out and tapped the back of his hand, drawing his attention back to her. "Really, Colm, I think we'd work well together."

"I hadn't planned on bringing more reporters onto this stage of the project, Anita."

"I understand, but the exposure would allow me to bring myself to the attention of the national bosses."

He appreciated a woman with ambition, and understood it. "I'll think about it, okay? As soon as we make a decision on who gets hired as lead producer."

"How is Radhika? She hasn't said much beyond what we discussed for her presentation."

He didn't detect anything but pure curiosity in the question. As far as he knew, no one at work knew they were seeing each other outside of the office. Respecting Radhika's wishes, he wanted to keep it that way as long as possible. "She seems to be doing well."

"We miss her down on our floor. She's a fabulous producer and you'd be lucky to have her."

"I know. Thanks. I'll let her know that you asked about her."

"Please do. The presentations are scheduled for Tuesday, right?"

"Yes."

"Can anyone sit in on them?"

He shook his head. "The only people present will be Dean, myself, Sylvia Moreno, and the presenter. Radhika can't watch Bella and vice versa."

Anita glanced around and then leaned back in. "I hear that if Bella's not selected for your position, they're going forward with the termination process."

"How did you hear that?"

Anita winked at him. "Confidential sources."

He made note to talk with Dean. "And any good reporter protects their confidential sources."

"Absolutely." She glanced at her watch. "My nephew's got a baseball game and I've got to get over there. Want to come with me and see a bit more of DC?"

He laughed. "No, thanks. I've got plans with my family."

"That's right. I heard you had someone here in town." She reached into her purse and pulled out her wallet. She dropped two twenties down on the table. "This should cover me. Thanks for the meeting."

"You're welcome. Have fun at the game."

"Thanks." She waved and headed out.

He sat there for a few more minutes while waiting for the server so he could get the check. He checked the time and saw he had another two hours before he was supposed to meet up with Kari, Marcus, and Nya. They were going to an ice show at the Verizon Center and then out for dinner as Nya's latest favorite production was touring.

The server came over and Colm gave her his card. He slipped Anita's twenties into his pocket. If nothing else, they'd be useful in buying Nya some tchotchke that Kari would roll her eyes over.

Later that evening, Colm was carrying Nya up the street to her house from the Metro stop. She'd fallen asleep on his shoulder as they took the train back from downtown. Kari and Marcus had planned on taking a taxi, but Nya wanted to ride on the train. She was still wearing the light-up necklace he'd gotten her, and Kari carried the bag full of other souvenirs. Marcus and she walked a few steps ahead of him. Marcus looked back over his shoulder. "You good with her?"

Colm grinned. "She's light as a feather. I may as well carry her back to her bed. No use in waking her up if we can help it."

"You can say that again."

They got back to the house and Marcus led the way up to

Nya's bedroom. Colm put her down on the bed and she squirmed, but stayed asleep. He slipped out the door and let Marcus get her tucked in.

Kari was down in the kitchen and she had a bottle of beer sitting out on the counter. "Thanks for coming with us tonight. I know dinner and a character-filled ice skating show aren't exactly scintillating Saturday night fun for a bachelor such as yourself."

Colm laughed. "Hey, one of the reasons I moved back here was so I could do more stuff with you guys."

"Yeah, but I wasn't expecting you to volunteer to go to this when I told you what our plans were."

"You never know where a story will come from."

Kari rolled her eyes and sipped from her own beer. Footsteps echoed down the staircase. Kari opened the fridge and pulled out another bottle of beer. Marcus came in and bent down to give her a kiss. "Thanks, babe."

She checked him with her hip. "Not in front of the baby brother."

Watching their easy way with each other had him thinking of Radhika. Would their ease in working together translate to coming home and relaxing together? Or would they just end up working even later into the night? Could they have this same level of togetherness outside of work? "You do know I'm only a year younger than you."

"Which means you'll forever be my baby brother."

"Thanks, you old crone."

She stuck her tongue out at him as she climbed up on one of the barstools. "So, tell me about Radhika. How's she doing?"

"She's well. She was out with friends today, otherwise I might not have been free to join you."

"You could have always invited her."

"I'm not sure if we're at the children's ice skating show stage of dating. I do have some standards." He winked.

"I'm proud of you. How's work going?"

"Good. I had a lunch meeting with Anita Lewis who's

looking to broaden her portfolio so she can be considered for a national position."

"How many meetings have you had like that?"

"So far just the one. Radhika set it up as they've been discussing issues for the presentation."

Marcus leaned back against the counter. "Radhika set it up?"

"Yeah. I don't have anything I particularly need help with at the moment, but Anita's offered her contacts among the Congressional staffers."

Marcus sipped his beer. "It's always good to have contacts with that group."

Kari nodded in agreement. "Will you have to give her air time if you take her help?"

"I wouldn't have to, but it's the right thing to do. We'll see what happens. If things go the way I hope on Tuesday, I'll talk with Radhika about the rest of the segments, so there may be an angle that we're not able to get on our own."

"I'm glad having her onboard is working out for you." She took another sip of her beer. "Don't screw it up."

"I appreciate your faith in me."

"We're planning another barbecue in two weeks. Ask her back. I'd love to see her again."

"Are Tracy and Missy coming back?"

"Tracy isn't."

She didn't say anything more, and when Colm looked over at Marcus, his brother-in-law only shook his head.

"I'll let her know."

"Good. Do you want some dessert? I've got cake left over from a party at work."

"What kind of cake?"

"Grocery store chocolate with white buttercream."

"Any flowers?"

She shook her head as she went over to the fridge. "You and your sweet tooth. I don't understand how you stay so skinny."

"It's contractual."

She pulled a large paper plate out of the fridge and he saw that under the plastic wrap, there were indeed icing flowers topping the buttercream frosting. Kari pulled down two plates and glanced over her shoulder at Marcus who shook his head. "I'll stick with the beer. Thanks."

Kari sliced two pieces from the cake, making sure the larger portion had almost all the flowers. She handed that and a fork to Colm and he dug in. There was something about chilled grocery store cake with the frosting containing insane amounts of sugar and fat that made his day. He'd periodically stop at the grocery store on his way home and buy a small birthday cake even though it wasn't his or anyone else's birthday.

While they ate, they spoke about their parents' upcoming visit to the city. "Have they talked with you about staying at your place?"

Colm shook his head and swallowed. "No. I thought they might be staying here."

"Mom hasn't said anything, and Dad mentioned something about hotel points."

"Well, I'm sure they've built up enough to say a week."

"If they wanted to spend them here. Mom's talked about visiting a resort in Thailand later in the year."

He pointed his fork between Kari and Marcus. "You know, if you guys wanted to get away for the weekend or something, I'd be happy to take care of Nya."

Husband and wife shared a look. "We've actually talked about that. Maybe later this summer. We haven't been to the beach by ourselves in a while."

"Whenever. Just give me enough lead time, and I'll block it out on my calendar."

"We'll get back to you. Thanks. I'll shoot Mom another email and copy you on it to see if they've made plans yet on where to stay."

"Great. I've got them on my calendar, but it will help to figure out dinners and such."

He finished up the cake and went over to the sink to wash the plate and fork. He kissed Kari on the cheek. "I need to head out. Thanks for dinner and dessert."

She gave him a hug. "Thanks for coming. I know Nya had a great time."

He turned to Marcus and gave him a one-armed hug. Marcus clapped his back. "I'm going to be downtown for a meeting tomorrow morning. Want to meet for lunch?"

Colm pulled out his phone and pulled up his work calendar. "It looks like I'm free. Does 12:30 work for you?"

"Perfect."

He typed in the lunch date. "I'll call you if anything comes up."

"Same here."

Kari walked him to the door and he waved goodbye as he hit the sidewalk.

Monday morning, as Colm walked into the office, he saw he beat Radhika in. He emailed Dean's assistant and was offered a short meeting slot if he was able to come up right away. He replied back taking it and then sent a quick email to Radhika to let her know where he was if she came in before he got back.

Dean looked up from his computer when he knocked. "Come on in."

Colm did and shut the door behind him. Dean noticed that and sat back in his chair with his fingers laced together over his stomach. "You didn't mention what this was about."

"Anita Lewis."

"Okay."

"Radhika's been in talks with her about the presentation. How hard would it be to bring her on to the project if Radhika is selected? She's a good reporter, and she's got a number of contacts with staffers on the Hill."

Dean nodded. "She interned and assisted on the political beat before she moved local and got the anchor job."

"Why didn't she continue with the political beat? She'd have moved up to national faster."

"Maybe, maybe not. There was a personality conflict with one of the hosts."

Colm sat back in his seat. "Anything I need to worry about?"

"No. She gets along well with the local team from what I've heard, other than the odd spat or two as you'd expect among competitive coworkers. I think this particular conflict was an isolated incident. Unlike some others I can name."

"Bella?"

Dean eyed him. "Any particular reason why you bring her name up?"

"Anita said word on the floor is that if Bella's not selected for the position, the termination process is going to continue. Can you give me an update?"

"No. We're not making any decisions until after tomorrow's presentations."

"Okay." He was unsure of what to say next.

Dean leaned back in his chair. "I have plans to submit this series when awards time comes. Live up to my expectations."

As Colm's expectations for himself were even heavier, he had every intention of doing exactly that. "I hope to hit the ground running as soon as we make a decision tomorrow. I have a target of having the first segment completed and ready to air in a month or so."

"Anything I should have a head's up on?"

"Not at this point. The first segment will mainly be introductory information. I've got a couple story threads that I'm going to be delving deeper into as the series progresses, but part of that will depend on who I can get to speak with on the Hill."

"Where Anita's contacts might come in handy."

"Yeah. Part of the problem, though, is that her experience isn't in meteorology, and I wouldn't want to cut her completely out of the story if I use her contacts."

Dean leaned forward and rested his arms on his desk. "That attitude is one of the reasons why I wasn't opposed to you starting this little project. I've talked with your previous bosses and bureau chiefs. One thing they all consistently mention is how you take mentorship seriously. This series could expand to be more. Maybe an incubation lab for upcoming talent. Something for you to think about."

Colm was a bit stunned. When he'd presented the idea of bringing Radhika on board to Dean, one of the arguments he'd used was grooming her for bigger assignments, but that hadn't been at the forefront of his mind. Turning this project into a mentoring lab intrigued him, but it was something to consider for later. "I'm still not sure where I could bring Anita on to give her air time."

"So maybe you don't use her on-air on this project. Give her a chance, though, and I'm sure you or she will find a way."

"I'll think about it."

"Think hard. Anything else?"

"Not right now."

Dean grunted, and Colm took that as his dismissal. Once back on his floor he headed for the office that had been temporarily assigned to Radhika and knocked. She scrambled to hide something on her monitor and then turned to him. He wasn't sure if the expression on her face was one of anger, confusion, or something completely different.

15

When Radhika got into work that morning, she skimmed through her email, picking out the most important ones. Colm had sent her a note that he was in a meeting with Dean, but didn't mention how long he'd be there.

She also found a response from an assistant at a non-profit she'd been cordially stalking. Colm had listed them as one of his top gets for the series. She opened the email, read it, and shot her fists into the air. The non-profit director would be happy to speak with Radhika, but her schedule was tight. Radhika sent back a message agreeing to a tentative meeting later in the week with the condition that she'd confirm late tomorrow afternoon. Her presentation was scheduled for right before lunch. She wasn't sure when Bella's was scheduled, but she hoped a decision would be made by the end of the day.

She was working on the timing for the first segment when her phone chirped with a text message. She picked it up and saw the beginning of a message from Hilda. Her friend rarely texted her during the work day, and if then, usually only on her lunch break. It was too early for that to be now. She opened her message app to read the full thing.

I'm not sure if you've seen this, and I'm sure it's nothing, but I figured you'd want to hear this from one of us rather than someone else who was telling you only to be a complete bitch.

Radhika had no clue what Hilda was talking about, but clicked on the link to a local gossip website. It was pictures of Colm with Anita. They were in an outside seating area, their head's close together as they talked over dishes of food. She read the story and confirmed her first thought that the pictures had been taken on Saturday.

IS THE HURRICANE HOTTIE FINDING LOVE WITH PAGEANT QUEEN-TURNED-NEWS ANCHOR?!?

The story reported that rumors had been heard about Colm dating a coworker. Her stomach twisted as she remembered the stories that had been written up after Vince's public break up with her. She knew there was nothing between Colm and Anita beyond work, but to have her boyfriend's relationship status speculated about in a tabloid had her heart sinking. If the gossip sites got their hands on who he really was dating, would she be able to handle it?

Radhika sat back in her chair and scrubbed her face with her hands. She was pretty sure neither she nor Colm had done or said anything at work that would be compromising. She knew he'd admitted to their past relationship, if a weekend together could be construed as a relationship, when he'd originally pulled her on board. But since then?

At work, he was the perfect coworker and rarely pushed the discussion into anything personal beyond confirming where and when they'd be meeting for their next date.

Who could have leaked a story like this?

And, of course, they'd immediately latch on to him with Anita. Her lips twisted. The shots were a little fuzzy, and she assumed they'd been taken with a phone rather than full camera rig. She rolled her shoulders, trying to work out the kinks she felt forming.

She went online and did a quick search of news stories about Anita, not because she didn't trust her, but Radhika wondered if there was anything in Anita's background that would have the paparazzi focusing more on her than on Colm.

That was the great thing about working for a news organization. Pretty much everything on the web could be considered research. She found the gossip stories about Anita's last relationship with a high-powered lobbyist who happened to be going through a divorce at the time. According to the last few stories, she'd been the one to break it off. And that had been a good three months ago. She hadn't been tied to one guy for more than a date or two since then.

There was a knock on her door, and she flipped the screen to the editing program she'd had open in the background. Turning around, she saw it was Colm. Unsure of what to say to him, she only stared.

"You okay?"

She nodded. Colm was a straightforward guy. If something was up, he'd tell her. Wouldn't he?

"I need to talk with you about something. My office?"

She blew out a breath. "Yeah, sure." She sent a quick text to Hilda, and then set her phone back into her purse and locked down her computer.

Colm motioned for her to close the door behind her, so she did and sat down. "What's up?"

"I went to see Dean about the lunch meeting I had with Anita."

"Oh?"

"Dean apparently is viewing our little project as a potential mentoring opportunity to move people up to national."

Radhika blinked. This really was the last thing she would have expected to hear. "That's...positive."

"Yes. I hadn't planned for it to be anything like that, but Dean's insistent. Anita and I talked about what she could add to the project, and she offered her contacts on the Hill for the story. Honestly, it's a tempting offer. I know you brought Anita to my attention, and I really appreciate it." He opened his mouth to continue, but let out a sigh before going on. "I'm going to have to inform Bella of the possibility of having Anita on board. I suggest you highlight what Anita could contribute in your presentation. Understand?"

Radhika nodded, but glanced over his shoulder and out the window to try and pull her thoughts together. She should tell him about the story so he wouldn't be blindsided. "She's good, and she has a way with the politicos. They respect her, and she isn't afraid to dig for a story. Screen time-wise, I'm not sure what she'd be able to do as this is very much your story and perspective. Depending on how much time you'd be willing to give up, we could have her do the interviews with a few staffers or legislators. Especially if she's the one who lands the contact. But I'd suggest that we start integrating her earlier than later, so her participation isn't a complete surprise for viewers."

"That's good and would probably appeal to Dean. Review the storyline we came up with, and pick out points where you think we'd be able to weave her participation in."

Radhika rubbed her thumb over her knee. "Colm, you should probably know something about Anita."

"Is it something that would be detrimental to the story? If so, I want to know. We've got the potential for good chemistry here, and I don't want to do anything to hurt that. This project's too important."

"No. I've worked with Anita before and she's really good and professional. She'd definitely be an asset. But, right before you came up, Hilda sent me a text. You guys are being talked about on the gossip sites."

Colm frowned. "Me and Hilda?"

"No. You and Anita. There's been speculation on one of the gossip sites that you're dating a coworker, and someone took pictures of you together on Saturday."

Colm's frown deepened, and he unlocked his computer. Within seconds he must have found the story. "Goddamn it. Radhika, I promise you, the only person I'm involved with outside of work is you."

Her gut twisted a bit. "I know. I was the one who set up that meeting. It's still jarring to see you possibly being in a relationship as a topic on a gossip site. I went through enough when my relationship with Vince imploded."

He came around the desk and crouched next to her chair. "I

can't help it if I end up on a gossip site, Radhika. I'm not seeking it out. I'm a public figure, though."

"I know, Colm." She bit her lip. "I...I have to think about this, okay?"

He frowned, but stood up. "Would you have a problem working with Anita on this? If it means there are more stories like this?"

"No. Just be up front with me if you need to work late with her or something."

"This is going to be a team environment which means you'll probably be working late with us if it comes to that. Are you okay with that?"

"Yes." She thought so. Hoped so.

Later that day, Colm knocked on Radhika's door. She was eating her lunch from a plastic bowl. "I guess that answers my question."

She swallowed. "What?"

"I was going to ask if you wanted me to bring you back anything for lunch."

"Where are you going?"

"I'm meeting Marcus at the sushi place down the street."

"Haru's?"

"That's it."

"Can you bring me some tofu ramen? It'll be my dinner."

"Sure."

She dug her wallet out of her purse and then handed him a bill. "Thanks."

He took it, enjoying the blush filling her cheeks as he slid his fingers against hers. "See you later. I'll text you if I'm going to be more than a couple of hours."

She gave him a thumbs-up and went back to eating. Shaking off the feeling that things weren't quite right between them, he headed out to meet up with Marcus. There was a crowd standing in the lobby area, but he didn't spot Marcus among them. He was halfway to the host stand when he heard his name called out. He turned back to the door and saw Marcus coming in. He waved and then continued forward to put his name down with the hostess.

"It'll be about twenty minutes."

"Thanks. The name's Colm."

She typed his name into the paging system and then handed him a buzzer. He worked his way back to where Marcus was standing in a corner. "How was the meeting this morning?"

Marcus shrugged. "Typical. They've started developing without clearly defining the end goals. They've got an idea of what they want, but there's only so much we can do without them being more specific."

"Did you tell them that?"

"Yes, and a few who were in the meeting seemed to get it from what I could read on their faces. Unfortunately for them, and us, they're not the ones in charge of the project."

Colm grinned. "Thank you for reinforcing why I never went into computers."

"Keep laughing, pretty boy. I'll send your sister after you. She's scheduled to work with these jokers in the next developmental stage."

Colm winced. "Should I be signing up for more babysitting time with Nya?"

"It wouldn't hurt. Oh, Kari wanted me to ask if you've talked with Radhika about the barbecue yet."

"Not yet. It's been a busy morning."

"So? You've got phones and there's this communication development called texting."

Colm shot Marcus a disgusted look. "I know. It's part of my slow build plan."

Marcus laughed and then stopped when Colm continued to stare at him. "Oh, you're serious."

"Yes."

"Dude. You've slept with her already. What's with the waiting?"

"She wants to go slowly with things being weird at work, and I want the right moment for her."

"You wait any longer and you're both going to be old and gray."

"You're a help."

Marcus stood straighter. "Want me to be a bigger help? Give me your phone."

"What?"

"Give me your phone." He held out his hand.

"No."

"Then text her yourself that you want to take her out to dinner. Tonight. Something fancy. You guys haven't done dinner yet, have you?"

Colm looked off to the side. "A couple times, but one time she got called in to sub for another producer."

He was saved from further berating by the buzzer going off. They made their way to the stand and handed in the buzzer. The hostess pulled a couple of menus from the side holder and led them to the table. Colm thought the discussion was done, but Marcus was only waiting until they were served their tea. "I mean it. Ask her to dinner. Right now. In fact, call her."

"No."

"Want me to call your sister? She'd love to hear this."

Colm scowled as he pulled out his phone. "You fight dirty."

"Bet your ass."

He selected Radhika's contact info and had it dial her personal cell phone. He got her voicemail. "Hey, Radhika. I was wondering if you wanted to go to dinner tonight. Are you free? I'm hoping so since you asked me to pick up ramen."

Marcus snorted at that. Colm discreetly flipped him off.

"Call me back when you get this."

"She asked you to pick up ramen?"

"Yes."

"You are pathetic. Truly pathetic."

"No, I'm a guy who respects the women he works with and tries not to muddy the waters too much with the one of them he happens to be dating."

"Your sister and I met at work and we kept those waters clear. We also managed to fuck like rabbits every chance we got."

Colm lifted his hands to his ears. "I'm not listening to this. I do not want to hear about my sister's sex life. Or yours for that matter."

"I'm telling you, man, the threat of discovery adds some spice to the mix."

"Can you shut up now?"

Marcus laughed and Colm ignored him to order his lunch.

Radhika got back from a meeting she'd been pulled into on an old story she'd worked on. Some new incidents had happened, and they wanted her input on what angles should be covered. She pulled out her phone to see if Rory had texted her back on a question she'd had, but saw she'd missed a call from Colm. She listened to the voicemail and frowned.

She didn't want anyone to overhear her, so she texted him back.

I'm free for dinner. Where are you thinking?

She set her phone down and opened her email to write a few follow up notes she'd thought of while walking back from the meeting.

There's this new place on 14th. Italian-South American fusion.

Her brows rose, but she texted back asking what time. She'd also heard about the restaurant and pulled up their website. If she needed to change for this place, she'd have to leave a little earlier than she'd planned on for the day. As she was perusing the menu, Colm's answer came back.

Eight?

She thought it over. It was a little later than she usually ate when she wasn't working the late shift, but if that was when reservations were available, she could work with that. She replied.

R: Reservations?

C: Not yet. Give me a minute.

She waited and pulled up some reviews on the food. Most of them were good, but a few said the service was slow. Not surprising with a newly-opened restaurant. This could go later than she was used to.

C: Open reservations at seven, and nine-thirty.

R: Seven.

She'd just leave work early. This was a date. While she could go in her work clothes, she shouldn't.

Made. See you when I get back?

She grinned. She still wasn't thrilled with the paparazzi coverage of him, but every time she knew they were going to be alone together, her body fizzed.

R: Yeah. I'll be here, but not for long. Have to go make myself pretty and all.

C: You're pretty enough as it is, but if you want to get hot, not that you need to do much to hit that, I'm all for it.

She snorted and replied that she'd see him when he got back. The rest of the afternoon went quickly. Colm came back from his lunch and carried a tub of ramen. "I know you said you wanted this for dinner, but I figured you could save it for lunch tomorrow."

"Thanks. I'll go throw it in the fridge." She got up and headed to the little kitchenette on their floor. One of the other reporters' assistants was in there getting a cup of coffee from the cartridge machine.

"Hey, Radhika."

"Hi, Julie." She took the marker hanging off the fridge and wrote her name and the date on the container before placing it in the fridge.

"So, are the rumors I'm hearing true?"

Radhika stood up. "What rumors?"

"About Colm and Anita?"

A little disturbed that she was now being asked about them, she closed the fridge and leaned on it. "What about them? I know Anita's talking to Colm about being part of the series he's doing."

Julie's face fell a little bit. "Oh. Well, you know people have been saying he's dating someone around here, but other than you, he hasn't spent much time with any of the women. And there's a pool going on who's going to be the first to bang him."

Radhika stood up straight. "What?"

"Yeah. I don't know who's in it, but I have a friend down in research who was telling me about it."

Well, that explained why she was getting so many offers from research for help on the series. "I haven't heard or seen him with anyone in particular."

"I'll let my friend know that she can hope."

Rather than saying anything she'd regret later, she waved goodbye to Julie and headed back to her office. She probably should warn Colm about the pool. But other than hearsay, she had no real evidence it existed. Though, she could absolutely believe it did. She resisted the urge to go down to research and stake her claim on him.

Wait. Her claim? Wasn't she supposed to be reluctant to get involved with a coworker? Maybe she should rethink dinner. When she sat down, she realized her hands were trembling. She closed her eyes and took five deep breaths.

Feeling marginally calmer, she glanced at the clock and decided to set the timer so she could leave work in time to get home, changed, and back up to the restaurant.

An hour later, as she was getting ready to leave, Colm stopped by. "What time do you want me to pick you up?"

"Pick me up?"

He glanced around, and lowered his voice and moved closer. She could smell the remaining traces of the body wash he must have used when he showered this morning. She wanted to burrow her nose into his chest, but before she could do so, he brought her attention back to his eyes. "Yeah. It's a date, and I pick you up."

"You don't have to. Traffic will probably be dicey."

"And I know there's not a Metro stop around the corner from the restaurant which means you either have to pay for a cab or take the train to a station where you can pick up a bus. Since I'm the one who asked you on the date, I'm not fond of either option. Besides, if I pick you up, we can spend more time together."

She blew out a breath. "Fine. Pick me up at six-thirty."

"Will do. I'll call you when I get close."

She patted his chest, partially to move him out of her way. It was ridiculously hard to step away from him. "I'll see you later, then."

16

*R*adhika checked herself out in the mirror, running her hand down her top and skirt. "Sexy, but not slutty."

With a slight adjustment, the pendant of the necklace she'd picked up in a little boutique in Georgetown rested right above her cleavage. She probably should have budgeted a little more time for her makeup since she hadn't done this much face in a while, but whatever.

She stroked on primer, eyeshadow, eyeliner, and mascara. Thankfully, with her complexion, she didn't require much more than that, blush, and lipstick. The blush took all of two strokes for each cheek, and then she lined her lips before painting on the red lipstick.

Now she was ready.

She slipped on the heels she'd selected and headed into the living room. Rory and Cecilia were on the couch watching TV with Rory's arm around Cecilia's shoulders. They'd ordered in dinner and the remains were sitting on the coffee table.

"I'm heading out in a little bit."

They looked over and both blinked. Rory was the first to talk. "Whoa. Who are you going out with?"

"Colm."

Cecilia dissolved into a giggle fit and Rory gently shook her. "Will you please stop that. If you keep giggling every time you hear his name, I'm going to start thinking you have a crush on him."

Cecilia shook her head, but didn't say anything else. Radhika grabbed her purse and phone before realizing she'd probably want a wrap tonight as the roller coaster weather of spring in DC had gone back to chilly. She went back into her bedroom and the closet where she kept her shawls hanging up. She selected one that had a mix of royal purple, blues, greens, and gold.

She heard her phone's alert going off and ran back into the living room. It was Colm saying he was at a light a block away. "He's almost here. Don't wait up for me."

Rory waved. "Like I ever would."

Radhika stuck her tongue out at him and headed out. Colm pulled up to the building's drive and got out to hold the door open for her. He bent and kissed her lips. "You look gorgeous."

She smiled. "Thank you. You're right on time." And gorgeous as well. He'd been wearing a suit at work and changed into slacks and a polo shirt. The color of the shirt picked out the gold highlights in his hair. He should have looked as if he'd walked off the pages of a preppy catalogue, but there was an edge to him. Maybe it was the line of his jaw and cheekbones. His features had been sculpted to be on TV.

He climbed in and buckled up before heading back into traffic. He did something with the stereo system and light jazz music filled the car. "I hope you like this."

"It's nice. How was traffic on the way over?"

"Not too bad. There were the usual backups of people trying to get out of town, but nothing I couldn't get around."

"Good to hear. Anything going on downtown we should be worried about?"

"Not that I've heard."

Cutting across town in a car to 14th from her place was going to be painful no matter what, but he went over to 7th, and up to M—muscling his way through the congestion by Gallery Place

—before cutting across to the west. He turned onto 14th and traffic, as she'd expected, was a bitch. They pulled up to the restaurant, and, thankfully, there was a valet on duty. He ran around the front of the car and handed Colm a ticket.

Radhika climbed out, and Colm came over to meet her. He rubbed her back, right above where it met her ass. She glanced up at him out of the corner of her eye, but his focus was on the door in front of them. He held it open for her and she stepped inside. The atmosphere was subdued, but not completely quiet. She saw a number of tables occupied by couples in various levels of dress. She pegged a few as tourists as they were wearing jeans and shorts with sneakers and sandals.

The host came around and shook Colm's hand. "I'm glad you were able to join us."

She shot him a look, but he only winked at her. "Thanks for taking the last-minute reservation."

"Happy to help out." The man grinned at Radhika as he waved his arm toward the back of the restaurant. "Follow me."

The host led them to a small alcove booth in the back where they were isolated even further from the other diners. "You requested red wine, yes?"

"Please."

When they were left alone, Radhika leaned into Colm. "What's going on?"

"A friend of Marcus's is one of the investors. I figured you deserved some romance. And he made it happen for me."

She blinked, then narrowed her eyes. "Romance?"

He reached out and ran his fingers over her bare forearm. "A beautiful woman who makes me laugh should be catered to. I'm sorry I haven't done as good a job as I should have if you're questioning me like that." His eyes met hers, and the burn in them lit a flame inside her. "I want to relearn everything about you and discover everything I missed last time."

His voice had lowered with every word he'd uttered until it reached deep inside of her and pulled. Hard. She drew in a deep breath, and when his gaze lowered, she realized that her breasts were pushing up against the neckline of the top. She couldn't regret it if it made him half as aroused as she was currently feeling. "You can't tell me you've been celibate since we were together."

"No. But you're still stuck in my head. I regret not getting in contact with you before moving here. I thought about it, though. When the opportunity to come to DC arose, you were part of the decision process for me."

He leaned in and kissed her neck. It was one of the spots he'd found during their weekend. She closed her eyes and leaned her head to the side. He sucked on the skin for a moment and the answering clench of her pussy had her gasping.

Someone cleared their throat.

Radhika blinked her eyes open. A waiter was standing in front of their table. With a wine bottle.

"Sir. Ma'am. The cabernet you requested."

"Thank you."

Colm's voice was gritty, but he was able to speak. Radhika wasn't sure if she was capable of any vocalizations that would be appropriate in polite company. She doubted it.

The server poured their wine and Radhika sipped hers. The notes of chocolate and spice in the dark red liquid felt even more decadent. Would she go home with him tonight?

Yes.

She felt her foundations shifting beneath her, but underneath that was the bedrock that she wanted to be with him. Tonight. He wasn't anything like Vince. He was focused on his career, yes, but not at the expense of his relationships with his family, friends, and colleagues. He took her concerns about appearances at work seriously. He turned her on to the point of combustion.

He was hers, and she was his.

She tried to focus on the menu, but the heat radiating from him, only inches from her, had her thinking of sheets, sweat, and sex. The speed at which she'd gone from interested to jump-on-me-aroused should have scared her, but she blamed it on prolonged exposure. This had been simmering for weeks. She reached down and rested her hand on his thigh.

He jumped. The tiniest bit, but she felt it. She was tempted to run her hand up to his crotch to see how aroused he was, but they were in public. Even if the tablecloth was draped discreetly over them.

His arm came around her shoulders and he leaned in so his lips touched her ear. "Play with fire and you're going to get burned."

She nuzzled her cheek against his chin. Skin smoothed by a razor caressed hers. "What if I want to get burned?"

He was close enough that she felt his lashes when his eyelids closed. "You're sure?"

"Mmhmm. But I want dinner first."

"Your wish. My command."

She squeezed his thigh and then brought her hand back up, tableside. "Are you good with small dishes?"

"Sure. Whatever you want?"

She selected some vegetable dishes that appealed.

He paused. "Are you a vegetarian?"

"Mostly. If you want meat, I'll share a chicken dish."

"All right."

Their waiter came over and took their order and the menus. "We're testing a new dessert service tonight. If you'd like, I can bring the menu over while you're waiting for your dishes to come out."

She looked up at Colm through her lashes. "Do you want to stay for dessert?"

"Are you in the mood for it?"

"I'm in the mood for something sticky."

The waiter coughed, but when she looked back at him, his face was completely neutral. "There is a caramel apple brûlée."

She laughed. "How about it, Colm?"

"Sure. Add that to the order. We'll share it." After the waiter left, Colm nuzzled her neck again. "You are being naughty."

"What are you going to do? Punish me?"

"I should." She felt his hand on her thigh, stroking the skin where her skirt ended. "What would you do if I brought you off right here? Or, maybe, I leave you dangling on the edge. Would that be punishment?"

She fought to keep her breathing under control. His words alone were taking her halfway there. If he got his fingers under her panties, she'd probably go off like a rocket. "You are devious."

"Don't you forget it." He pressed kisses along her neck. "When it comes to having you in my bed again, Radhika, I'm going to be ruthless."

Of this she had no doubt. She opened her eyes in time to see one of the servers coming by with their first dish. Colm didn't remove his hand until the server left. She wasn't going to let him get away with this.

Two hours later, Colm handed Radhika back into his car. The look she shot him burned through any remaining reservations he may have had. A flash briefly blinded him, but when he looked over, a man was taking a photo of his girlfriend who was posing in front of the restaurant's sign.

Colm ran around the car and slipped the valet a ten. The traffic hadn't lightened up at all as people were heading to the restaurants and clubs farther up. He turned onto the first street that would let him head east. Radhika sat silently in the passenger seat, looking out the window.

"Are you sure about this?"

She turned back to him and smiled. "Yes."

He let out a breath and held out his one hand. She stared at it for a moment before she slipped hers into it. He felt something center inside of him and relaxed.

The drive back to his apartment building went smoothly, as he'd learned which streets were quieter, and therefore quicker, than others. He parked in his spot. He saw Radhika reaching for the door. "Hold on."

He ran around to the other side and opened the door for her, helping her out. She smiled up at him. "Thank you."

"I do try to be polite."

"And you manage it so well."

Colm slipped his arm around her waist. "Remember how I told you I'd been in boarding school for a bit?"

"Yeah."

He led her over to the elevators, enjoying the feel of her body moving under his arm. "Well, one of the required courses was a semester on etiquette."

She held up her hand to her mouth, but he still heard the laughter. "Really?"

"Yep. It's actually come in handy a few times when I've been out with the network big wigs."

"I'm sure there's a lot of call for etiquette at golf courses."

"Oh, ye of little faith. It was high-dollar charity events. You need to be able to tell if you're accidentally stealing someone's bread knife during the fish course."

She looked up at him and then doubled over with laughter.

"I'm not kidding." The elevator doors opened and he guided her inside, patting himself on the back for making sure she didn't trip even as she continued to laugh at him. He stole a quick kiss from her, enjoying the feel of her laughter on his lips.

"I know you're not, which makes it even funnier." He watched as she tried to catch her breath once she finally stopped laughing. Like any man could resist looking at the expansion of her chest. Some guys were about the breasts, others liked ass, but for him, Radhika was the whole package. What really turned him on, though, was how she wasn't afraid to laugh and be natural around him.

He wasn't blind to his looks, so he knew he'd had an easy time with women over the years, but a lot of them were as interested in what he could do for them as they were in him as evidenced by the most recent spate after the magazine feature.

Radhika didn't care about that. If she wanted something, she was going to go for it on her own. She made him want to conquer the world so he could lay it at her feet, and not because she requested or demanded it like his latest girlfriends would have. He wanted to give her every opportunity she needed to achieve her dreams.

The doors opened at the lobby, and one of his neighbors was standing there. The woman held a little fluffy black and white dog in her arms.

"Oh, hello, Colm." She stared at Radhika who still let out periodic giggles.

"Amy. This is my friend Radhika."

Amy smiled at Radhika, but held up the dog as an excuse for not shaking hands. When the doors opened again on their floor, she stepped out first and waved one hand from under the dog. "Bye, Colm. See you later."

Colm put his arm around Radhika to guide her to his apartment, but she was stiff in place.

When he looked down at her, she batted her lashes and waved one hand. "Bye, Colm. See you later." The volume was *sotto voce*, but he clearly heard the sarcasm.

"What?"

"If you can't see what just happened, I'm not about to enlighten you."

He bent down so they were eye to eye. "I know perfectly well what happened, and I'm choosing to ignore it. The woman who I want to be with is standing right next to me, and, I'm hoping, is still planning to join me in my apartment."

Radhika pursed her lips for a moment not breaking eye contact, then nodded. "As long as you are aware."

"You don't have to fight anyone to get me into your clutches."

He caught her narrowing her eyes at him, but like Amy's flirting, chose to ignore it. He pulled out his keys and opened the lock on the door. Radhika came in and he closed the door behind her. He reached for her wrap, enjoying the feel of silken fabric and even silkier skin. "Would you like something to drink?"

Radhika turned around and looked at him. Cupping his jaw with her hands, she looked at him. He was a little worried she had changed her mind, but if she did, she did, and he'd drive her home. Instead, she surprised him.

"I want to be with you very much, but I need to know you won't tell anyone at the office. All right?"

He lifted his own hand to stroke her skin where neck met shoulder. "That's fine. Work is work. Home is home. Whatever happens is between us."

She lifted up until her lips met his. Her hands moved down his body, her fingers slipping into the waistband of his slacks. She worked them until they hooked under his shirt and pulled it out. He deepened the kiss, tangling her tongue with his.

The heat that had been simmering between them all night flared back to life. He felt her nails rake the skin of his back and he shuddered. "Bedroom. Now."

"Yes."

He bent and lifted her. Faster. He needed her faster. He dropped her onto his bed and gave thanks that he'd thought ahead enough to make the bed with fresh sheets when he'd gotten home. She bounced a bit and giggled.

Turned on more from that light sound than he'd ever thought possible, he followed her down, covering her body with his. She hummed and kissed his jaw before claiming his lips. "Take your shirt off."

He went up onto his knees and yanked the shirt over his head. When he bent back down to kiss her, he slipped his hand under her top. His palm met her lace-covered breast and she sighed.

Letting his fingers trail up and down her side, he discovered the zipper underneath her armpit. He tugged on the tab and pulled it down. Slipping his hands underneath the hem, he pushed it up. She raised her arms over her head. He tossed the top off to the side.

Her bra was a wine-colored lace, and he could see her hard nipples through it. He bent his head, fastening his lips on one of them. He sucked a bit, but the lace interfered.

It must have done something for her because she gasped. He unzipped her skirt, and kneeled up on the bed so he could skim it down her long legs.

Her panties matched the bra and looked gorgeous against

the burnished dark gold of her skin. He tossed the skirt in the general direction of the top, and trailed one hand from her hip up to her collarbone.

"You're unbelievable."

She grinned back at him. "So are you."

17

*R*adhika couldn't believe she was here. She hadn't planned on it, but it was happening. She pushed on Colm's shoulder until he rolled over and was laying on his back. She lifted one leg over and straddled him. His abs were even harder than when they'd last been together. He reached up and brushed her hair behind her ears. "Really, really gorgeous. Thanks for coming back with me."

Even beyond the sexy burn filling her body, those simple words warmed her. She bent down until her lips were millimeters from his. "I'm glad to be here."

She kissed his smile, opening her mouth so her tongue could play with his. His hands ran up and down her back, stopping briefly to unhook her bra. The straps fell down her shoulders and she wiggled them until they hit her elbows. She pulled one off and then the second, tossing the bra away from the bed.

Colm curled up effortlessly, forcing her to sit up. He captured one hard nipple in his mouth. She threaded her fingers through his hair and rocked against him. He propped himself up on one hand and slid the other down the front of her panties. His fingertips brushed her clit and she shuddered. "Yes."

He pressed his fingers in and she ground down on him. He sucked even harder on the nipple. Her breath caught as she realized she was at the edge of orgasm. He must have felt the change in her body as he bit down on her nipple while he rubbed her clit.

The orgasm rushed over her and she clutched him to her.

As it eased, he wrapped his arms around her and rolled her over so she was the one lying on the bed. He kissed the crook of her neck and stroked his hands down her body. She shuddered as residual waves rocked her system. "Colm. I need you."

He bent his head and kissed her. "Same. I need to get protection first. Be right back."

She nodded as she tried to catch her breath. As she stared up at the ceiling, she could hear him moving around. Music came on the stereo system. Something low and sensual.

She started to lift herself up to see where he was, but he climbed back onto the bed before she could move more than her shoulders.

She hummed when she realized he'd gotten rid of his pants and had put on the condom. She shifted her legs, opening herself to him.

Laughing, he rested his forehead on hers. "Panties, first, I think."

"What?" Then she remembered she'd never gotten around to taking off the panties with the bra.

She scooted up the bed and reached down to get them off. Her fingers tangled with his, but he managed to slip them down her legs and toss them away.

This time when she shifted her legs, he settled in between them. His cock was as hard and ready as she remembered it. She hitched her leg up over his hip and pulled him close, encouraging him.

"I kind of thought you'd want foreplay."

"What do you think that orgasm was?"

"An appetizer?"

"Foreplay later. Sex now."

His laugh was decidedly strained, but he reached down and positioned himself before pushing in. He took it slow. She wasn't sure if it was him being courteous or because it just felt that goddamned good. Either way, she didn't care so long as he kept it up.

Radhika wrapped both arms around his neck and groaned as he got all the way in. She shifted her hips and felt him slip in that extra bit. Her breath caught as her inner muscles rippled in reaction.

He growled.

Colm actually growled.

She clenched down on him even harder.

The reaction that forced was mind blowing. He pounded into her. She pushed back into him, needing all he'd give her. His hand slid down her stomach and he pressed the heel of his palm down just above where their bodies met. She closed her eyes and let her head fall back. The feel of him surrounding her, in her, was everything. The first orgasm had only been a small taste.

When he began rubbing his palm against her, her body couldn't take it all and she orgasmed again.

This time she shouted as she came. He bent down and she felt his teeth against her shoulder as he followed her after a few more short thrusts.

Sweat trickled from his body to hers, dampening the blanket beneath her. She threaded the fingers of one hand through his hair and held him close. She didn't want to let him go, and she wasn't sure what that meant. The idea of it only being a fling drifted further away.

She pressed a kiss to his temple when he moved.

He nuzzled her nose with his. "You okay?"

"Yeah. I can't stay, though."

"Why not?"

"First, I have no clothes here. Second, I hate getting up earlier than I have to, so I don't want to leave here at five so I can go to my apartment and then get back up to work on time."

"Do you have to leave right now?"

"No."

He kissed her and she was tempted to slide back into the

fantasy of being with him always. Fantasies had to end. Didn't they?

"Good. Give me a second." He pulled out of her and she shuddered at the feeling.

She turned her head so she could watch his ass as he walked away and disappeared around a corner. She heard the flush of the toilet and running water, realizing he had a master suite bathroom. She sat up in bed as he returned with a wet wash-cloth. He held it out to her.

She took it and wrapped her hand around his neck, drawing him closer so she could kiss him. "Thanks. I'll be right out."

She headed to the bathroom and after taking care of what she needed to, she looked at herself in the mirror. Dazed eyes, puffy lips, and hearts and stars exploding all around her. She was sunk. "What are you going to do?"

18

*L*ater the next morning, Radhika smoothed her hand down the jacket of her suit. She rarely pulled it out, but with Colm, Dean, and Sylvia Moreno judging her, she needed all the armor she could muster.

Dean's assistant had assured her the projection unit was prepped. She knocked on the door of the conference room. Dean opened the door for her and gestured to the front of the room. Colm and Sylvia were seated off to the side of the lectern where a laptop sat.

"You're prepared for a fifteen-minute presentation, correct?"

"Yes, sir."

Dean walked to the other side of Colm and sat down. "We're ready when you are, Radhika."

She walked over to the laptop and signed onto the network. Moments later she brought up the presentation. She began with the storyboard for the series outline.

"Based on my conversations with Mr. Jones, I envision this as a ten-episode weekly series. You can see I've listed the main arc of each episode, the proposed locations, and the suggested interviews. So far I've been able to confirm interest with roughly a third of the guests, primarily from the first three episodes."

She flipped to the next slide. "Based on available ratings

from similar specials, this is the audience I believe we can reasonably expect." Her graphic showed the broad audience size, along with demographic breakdowns and potential target advertisers.

"I have a short clip I'd like to show you."

Colm jumped up. "I'll get the lights." She tried not to focus on the movement of his ass beneath his dress pants as he jogged to the back of the room and turned them off.

Radhika waited until he returned to his seat before hitting play. She'd only lightly edited the interview she'd done with a public relations director last week. Their focus on sustainable energy generation in city environments could have been drier than the Dust Bowl, but the director was a young woman who was telegenic and passionate about her topic. After five minutes, the video ended.

Colm once again went for the lights. He had a huge grin on his face when coming back and she couldn't help but grin back at him. She had this.

She went through the rest of her presentation, and closed the laptop to take questions. For a moment, she thought Colm would be the first to speak, but Sylvia leaned forward.

"This presentation was very comprehensive, Ms. O'Leary. How well would you say you worked with Mr. Jones?"

Beating back a blush as she was sure the question was meant as professionally as possible, she cleared her throat. "I would say we worked well together. Will work well together."

Dean sat up. "I understand from Colm that you two had a previous relationship. Would this interfere at all with your completion of this project?"

Radhika kept her gaze glued on Dean. "Not at all, sir. I hold Mr. Jones in the highest esteem. It would be an honor for me to work with him on this project."

Sylvia brought Radhika's attention back to her with a movement of her hand. "Be honest, Ms. O'Leary. What are your goals for this project?"

The words rushed out of her. "I want it to win awards." She blinked. Until Sylvia asked the question, she hadn't realized how badly she wanted that. She met each of their gazes. "It *will* win awards."

Sylvia nodded and sat back. Dean stroked his chin and looked at Colm. "Any questions from you?"

"A few." He walked her through points of the story arc. They weren't for form's sake and had her rethinking the positioning of some possible story elements, but he was also talking with her as if she already had the job.

When she finished answering his last question, he smiled. "Thank you, Radhika."

It would be so not professional to run over to him for a hug and kiss. Right? She shook each of their hands, Colm last. He squeezed her hand a little harder than Dean had, and stroked his thumb across the back of it.

No melting. No melting.

Her knees managed to hold themselves together long enough for her to get back to her temporary office.

She let out a deep breath and put her head down between her knees. A knock sounded, and she lifted up, grazing her head on the edge of her desk. "Ow."

"Damn. I'm sorry. Are you okay?"

Colm. She let out a sigh as he wrapped his hand around the back of her head and massaged it. She leaned back into the caress, letting herself sink into the ministration. After a few minutes, and having mentally drifted off to a beach where they were the only occupants, she felt a kiss on her forehead. By the time she opened her eyes, he had stepped away. "Better?"

"A bit." She studied him. His hands were in his pockets and his shoulders were squared off. "Are you okay?"

One shoulder jerked. "I'll be fine once Bella's presentation is over."

"I know it's this afternoon, but I never heard what time." She'd resisted finding out so she wouldn't contemplate hanging out by the meeting room to find out what happened.

"One o'clock. Sylvia, Dean, and I are going to lunch." He glanced at his watch. "In fact, I should be meeting them downstairs right now."

She shooed him away with her hands. "Go. I'll talk with you later."

He went behind the desk and crouched down next to her, taking one of her hands into his. "Whatever happens, we're good, right?"

Her breath caught in her chest. She wanted to rake her fingers through his hair, but it wouldn't do to muss him up before meeting with Dean and Sylvia. Needing some connection, she cupped his jaw.

"We'll work it out." There was a churn in her gut. She may have nailed the presentation, but that didn't mean everything was perfect now.

He must have understood because he lifted her hand to his lips and kissed her knuckles. "I'll see you later."

"Later. Have a good lunch."

After lunch, Colm stopped by his office to do a quick check of his email. They had about ten minutes before Bella's presentation. Unfortunately for him, no news that she had cancelled. He had to keep an open mind.

Radhika had killed her presentation, though. Sylvia had said at lunch that if the assignment with him didn't work out, she'd be interested in pulling Radhika in on a few of her own projects she was producing. Pride and fear made for an uneasy mix with the burger he'd been eating.

He answered a few quick questions and let the local evening news broadcaster know he'd be available to comment on the high activity of the past cyclone season for the Pacific as part of a story they were doing on a local relief effort.

His calendar popped up a reminder that the presentation was starting in five minutes. He grabbed his notebook and pen and jogged down to the meeting room. Both Dean and Sylvia were already there, but no sign of Bella.

He let out a short breath and went to sit by his fellow panelists.

"Colm, I'll take point with this presentation, if you don't mind. I have the least history with Ms. DiNunzio."

Colm nodded at Sylvia. "I'd appreciate it."

"She understands the expectations of the presentation?"

"I believe so. I sent her the same instructions I sent to Radhika, and she didn't send me any follow-up questions."

Sylvia's brows rose, but before she could say anything, Bella strode into the room. Behind her was a young man who slipped to the side and sat down by the doorway. He struck Colm as vaguely familiar.

Colm frowned, but before he could say anything, Sylvia took the lead and addressed the man. "I'm sorry, but this is a closed meeting. You'll have to leave."

Bella paused in the middle of the room. "I want him here."

"No." Sylvia left it at that as she stared at Bella.

The man didn't acknowledge them, but didn't leave until Bella turned back to him and nodded.

Bella continued to the front of the room and plugged a USB drive into the computer. She faced them and smiled. It was a professional, practiced, and plastic smile.

The area between his shoulder blades twitched.

"Ms. DiNunzio, you understand you are here to present your vision of the series Mr. Jones has proposed. You will be judged on the content as well as your presentation skills. Do you have any questions for the panel before you begin?"

"No. I understand. I believe you will have no choice but to offer me the position."

The poison that dripped from the words made Colm want to leave the room, but Sylvia placed her fingertips on his thigh below the table. She'd also heard the threat. He slowly let out his breath as Bella began her presentation.

It was pedestrian and didn't enhance anything he'd already done in the packet he'd sent her. As she droned on, he began to relax.

She paused and turned to them. "Are there any questions at this point?"

Sylvia looked to Dean and Colm. Colm shook his head. Sylvia leaned back in her seat. "I do have a few, Ms. DiNunzio."

She ran through many of the questions she'd had for Radhika. Once again, Bella's answers were a distant second to Radhika's. Sylvia ended with her question of goals.

Bella turned her attention to Colm, and, once again, the skin on his back tightened. "I'd very much enjoy working with Mr. Jones. I believe he has a bright future ahead of him and I can contribute to his success."

Sylvia nodded. "Is there anything else you'd like to add to your presentation?"

Bella grinned. "I'm pleased you asked." She went to the laptop and began opening files that appeared on the screen. "As you know, this company has a strict policy against romantic fraternization of coworkers. As you can see from this report filed soon after he started, Mr. Jones informed Human Resources of a relationship of that sort with Radhika prior to his employment. However, what he has failed to disclose is the fact they have continued that relationship in direct violation of the policy. I believe Radhika is using her connection with Mr. Jones to unduly influence him to advance her career."

Photos of the two of them on their dates outside the office popped up. There was even a picture of them kissing as the doors to his apartment building's elevator closed. Someone had followed them from the restaurant.

He sprang out of his chair. "What the fuck?"

Bella tilted her head. "Are you denying your relationship with her? Well, here's some video from this morning." Somehow, some way she had gotten video of the conversation he'd had with Radhika in her office just after her presentation.

"That's an invasion of privacy."

Bella's smile sharpened. "No, that's a violation of company policy. You have no choice but to give me the position and fire Radhika. If you don't, I will make sure this video and all my supporting evidence is released to the other stations by this afternoon. She will never work in this town again."

The words of cartoon villains hung in the air, and Colm

couldn't draw a breath through the tightness of his chest. This was unbelievable. He—they were being blackmailed by this viper of a woman.

"What is your problem with Radhika? Since I've started, everyone who has worked with the two of you has made a point to tell me about your vendetta against her."

Bella's face hardened. "I was supposed to be the one Vincent Rizzoli brought with him to New York. She got her hooks into him, and he left me for her. Her. I had the connections. I had the experience to make him great. But he started dating her."

Colm rubbed his temples. This was about that absolute shit-head, Vince? Next time he was in New York, he was going to punch the asshole.

"You realize that Radhika had to quit her job after he dumped her? Neither of you are in New York with him."

"He has great talent and realized a nobody like her would never be able to support him in achieving his dreams. She should be punished for distracting him." Bella was damn near foaming at the mouth in her hatred for Radhika. "You should have known better. She drags down the talent. You can go far. I can help you."

Before he could respond, Sylvia reached up and gripped his forearm. He looked down and she shook her head. He sat down. Sylvia turned to Bella. "Thank you for bringing this to our attention, Ms. DiNunzio. We'll have to take this new information under consideration as we decide."

"When do I start? I can move my things into the office next to Mr. Jones immediately."

There was no way in hell he was working with this delusional woman. "I quit. I refuse to be a party to this." He got up and strode out of the room.

Dean shouted after him, but he ignored his boss and headed to Radhika's office. He caught sight of the man who'd accompanied Bella in to the presentation. He went over and grabbed the guy by the shirtfront. "You were at the restaurant last night, weren't you? You were the guy who took our picture."

The man held up his hands. "I was only doing the job I was hired for. Chill out."

Before Colm could do anything further, someone gripped his shoulder. He turned his head and found Dean standing behind him. "Leave him alone. We need to talk."

"No. I quit. Remember?" He pushed the guy back and headed once again to Radhika's. She wasn't in her office. He had no clue where she was and he needed to get out of here. He'd text her asking her to meet with him.

He went to his office and began packing things into his bag. Dean found him there.

"What are you doing?"

Colm glared at him. "What do you think? I'll send you my official resignation letter later. I'm still within the probationary period, so I'll let my agent know the position didn't work out and she should make the split as amicable as possible."

"You're being an idiot. Bella more than crossed the line."

Colm slammed the last award he'd won down on his desk. "What does it matter? I'm seeing Radhika and I plan to continue seeing her so long as she'll have me. I'm not going to fuck this up."

A gasp had them both turning to the door. Radhika stood there, her face drained of color. "What have you done?"

"Radhika, wait."

She shook her head and headed out. Colm pushed past Dean and raced after her. The doors to the elevator were closing by the time he reached them. "Goddamn it."

He ran around the corner to the stairwell and raced down to the lobby. His chest bellowed as he tried to draw in air as he headed to the elevators. He was bent, hands on his knees, as the doors of the one he assumed Radhika had gotten on opened. She was in the middle of the pack of people getting out. He grabbed her arm, but she pulled away.

"No. You do not get to touch me. What were you thinking?"

People stepped away from them, and out of the corner of his eye, Colm saw one of the guards lift her head. Denise. Shit. "Can we talk about this somewhere else?"

"No. I have nothing to say to you. I told you I didn't want people finding out about us."

"Bella has photos and video. She showed them as part of her presentation."

Radhika stepped back as if he'd made to hit her, and he realized he'd raised his voice. Fuck.

"Please. Can we go somewhere else and talk about this?"

Denise came over. "Do we have a problem here?"

Radhika shook her head. "No. You won't have any more problems because of this."

Something inside of him died at her words. "Radhika?"

She shook her head again and walked to the entrance. He made to go after her again, but Denise moved in front of him. "Leave her alone."

"I need to make this right."

Denise stared at him. "You can't do that now, so leave her alone. Got it?"

He watched her walk out into the sunshine. Without him. "Yes."

19

*R*adhika was sitting on her couch watching one of the shopping channels when a knock came from the door. "Rory. Get the door."

"I'm working on applications. You get it."

"Please."

"Get off your ass."

She grumbled, but climbed off the couch. Since she wasn't expecting anyone, she checked the peephole first. Groaning, she hit her head against the door before opening it. "Rory called you, didn't he?"

"Yep. What's going on?"

"Nothing. You can go home."

Stacey pushed past her and looked at the television. "Shopping channels? Really? What the hell happened, Radhika?"

"Nothing."

"You watching shopping channels is not nothing. Tell me you haven't bought anything."

Radhika winced. There may have been shoes. Stacey came over and hugged her. "Come on. We're going to meet the girls for dinner."

Radhika looked down at the leggings and t-shirt she'd changed into when she'd gotten home. "I'm not going out."

"Yes, you are. Rory, grab her coat for me."

Rory came out of his room and tossed the jacket Radhika had left on the back of one of the dining room chairs at them. Radhika scowled at him. "Traitor."

"You wouldn't tell me what the hell happened, so I called in reinforcements. If you won't tell me, you get to tell them."

Stacey wrapped the jacket around Radhika's shoulders until she had no choice but to put her arms into the sleeves. Stacey grabbed Radhika's purse and herded her out of the apartment as soon as Radhika slipped her feet into the pair of flats she had next to the door. "I'll call you when we're heading back, Rory."

"See you." He closed and locked the door behind them.

Radhika crossed her arms as they waited for the elevator. "This is called kidnapping, you know."

Stacey pulled Radhika's phone out of her purse. She brought up the notification screen and her brows rose. Holding the phone out so Radhika could see it, she pointed to the pertinent notification. "And this is called avoidance. Why are there over ten texts from Colm that are unread?"

"None of your business." The elevator doors dinged. Thankfully, the car was empty.

Stacey came in after her. The ride down was accomplished in silence. Expecting to have to hail a cab or something to get to wherever they were having dinner, she was surprised to see Jorie sitting in the driver's seat of a car. "What's going on?"

Jorie leaned over and pushed open the passenger side door. "Get in. We're going to dinner."

Stacey prodded her in the back.

"I'm going. I'm going." Radhika climbed in and buckled up.

As soon as Stacey was in the backseat, Jorie pulled out into traffic. "Hilda's making dinner, and we're going to her place. You are going to spill what's going on with you."

Radhika opened her mouth, but Jorie held up a hand. "Save it until we get there. Your brother usually doesn't text all of us to come deal with you."

"I'm going to kill him."

Stacey piped up from the back seat. "No. What you are going

to do, after we get you home, is thank him for being such a nosy, caring brother."

"I wanted to be by myself."

Jorie glanced over. "Stop wallowing. You're better than this."

Radhika looked out the window as they crossed over the Potomac. A plane was coming in to land at Reagan National. She stared at it as it loomed closer and closer, then Jorie pulled off onto the Parkway. They wound their way through Arlington and Alexandria until they turned onto the street where Hilda and Erin lived. Jorie managed to find a parking spot a few doors down.

They climbed out of the car and Radhika followed Jorie and Stacey to the door. She gave brief thought to making a run for the Metro, but with her luck the trains would be delayed and Jorie would drag her back here.

Jorie knocked and Erin opened the door. She held the door open for them, and Jorie and Stacey gave her a hug as they went in. Radhika stepped in and waved. "Hi. Sorry for the intrusion."

Erin reached up and gathered her into a hug. Not wanting to be a complete bitch, Radhika gave her a quick squeeze and stepped back.

"Hilda's in the kitchen. Dinner should be ready soon."

"Thanks." She followed Erin into the dining area that was attached to the kitchen. Stacey was at the fridge opening a bottle of water. Jorie had leaned against one of the counters and already had a glass of wine in hand. Hilda looked over her shoulder from where she stood at the stove. "Do you want water or wine?"

"Wine."

"Good choice. Jorie, can you pour her a glass?"

Jorie set her glass down and poured one for Radhika. As she handed it over, she stared at Radhika. "Okay. What's going on?"

Knowing she couldn't get out of here without telling them everything, she took a seat at the table. "We had the presentations today."

Stacey smiled. "Oh, yeah. How did you do?"

"I thought I rocked it. However, I stopped by Colm's office after Bella's presentation and caught him telling Dean we had been seeing each other."

Her four friends stared at her, varying levels of confusion on their faces. It was Erin who finally spoke the question that seemed to be on all their tongues. "So?"

"He wasn't supposed to tell anyone that we were seeing each other. Not only does the company have a policy against seeing coworkers, I don't want anyone thinking I'm using him."

Hilda tapped her wooden spoon on the side of the skillet. "Does he think you're using him?"

"I don't know. I just left, but he chased me down in the lobby."

The confusion was replaced by exasperation. Stacey came over and sat down by her. "What did you say?"

Radhika closed her eyes and let her head fall back. "That I couldn't believe he told Dean and that I couldn't talk to him about it."

A clank of silverware had her opening her eyes. Jorie had slammed forks and knives down next to her. "You screwed up."

"No, I didn't. He did. Now if I get the job, everyone's going to think it's because I've slept with him. I don't fuck guys to get ahead, despite what Vince told people."

Hilda came over and dished out the dinner she prepared. "My God. I knew Vince was a dickbag, but I didn't realize you had become such a cynical bitch thanks to him."

Radhika glared at Hilda who glared right back at her.

"Listen, you. From what little you've told us, Colm seems like a good guy. He wanted to talk this out with you, but you refused. You could have been gracious, and open minded, and fucking listened to his side of the story."

Radhika leaned back as Hilda leaned into her. "I—"

Hilda held up a hand. "No. No more of this shit. You had your little running scared hissy fit and blew up at him. If you're at all lucky, he's going to give you a chance to grovel."

"I did nothing wrong."

"Like fuck you did. Yes, you caught him telling your boss that the two of you had a relationship. When he tried to explain, you acted like a child and shut him down in front of your coworkers. You. Fucked. Up."

Jorie was nodding along. "Big time."

Radhika scowled at Jorie who only stared back at her.

Hilda reached out and placed her hand on Radhika's arm. "You can't live your life choosing fear." She glanced at Erin and smiled at her. "Erin and I have managed to build a relationship the three of you are helping us to celebrate in a few months. That doesn't mean we haven't had our issues. We worked through them. We talked about them like adults. And we consciously chose against fear. In the end, anyway. What you and Colm have could be something very special."

Hilda looked at Stacey and Jorie, who each nodded, before turning back to Radhika. "We've watched you bloom in the last few weeks. You've been in stasis since Vince. Colm helped you break free of that. Don't let it slip through your fingers."

She let out a sigh. Now that her initial rage had cleared, followed by some well-deserved wallowing, she knew she had fucked up. Horribly. She closed her eyes and whispered. "You're right."

Hilda put the skillet back on the stovetop and came back. "Call him. Tell him to come over here, if he's willing to listen to you."

"I can't."

Stacey nudged her foot. "God, girl, get some balls. Call him."

Radhika pulled out her phone and found a new text notification. It was from Colm. All it said was *Call me.* "Goddamn it."

"What?"

She showed the phone to Stacey. "Oh." Stacey passed the phone first to Jorie who gave it to Hilda.

Hilda took Radhika's hand in hers and put the phone in it. "You know what you need to do."

Fear or bloom? If she put herself out there, and he rejected her, would she wither again? She glanced at each of her friends.

No. They wouldn't let her. She hadn't realized how much she'd lost herself after Vince dumped her. Working for Bella hadn't helped matters. But she was the one who had buried herself. She wouldn't let herself get buried again. "Yeah. After dinner. I want some privacy for this."

~

Colm tipped back his beer as he watched Marcus grill up some burgers. Marcus looked over when he stood. "You okay, man?"

"Will be as soon as I get another of these." He didn't miss the worry on his brother-in-law's face, but he did ignore it.

He walked into the kitchen to find Kari getting something out of the fridge. "Can you get me another beer while you're at it?"

Kari's lips pursed, but she did as he requested. He twisted the top off and tossed it into the garbage can. "Burgers should be ready in a bit."

"Good. Are you going to tell me what's going on?"

"How about I have no clue?"

Kari pointed at the breakfast bar. "Sit and tell your big sister all about it."

Colm let out a breath. He knew if he didn't, she'd call up their parents—and probably wake them up—to get him to talk. He sat down on the barstool and leaned his elbows on the counter. "Did I tell you that in order to have Radhika work with me on a special project, she had to do a presentation?"

"No. What about it? She didn't bomb it, did she?"

"No. She rocked it. The reason she had to do the presentation was because her boss, Bella, had filed a complaint about Radhika's original placement on the project. She wanted it for herself."

"Oh. Is that unusual?"

Colm lifted a shoulder. "Special projects happen all of the time. I asked for Radhika to be assigned and Dean backed me up. Once the complaint was filed, though, we went by the book to address it. The problem is that Bella filed the complaint after having a complete meltdown outside of my office after she found out I was out for a working lunch with Radhika. Bella's got a number of complaints filed against her, and this meltdown led to her being temporarily committed to a psych ward."

Kari's eyes were huge. "Whoa."

"Yeah. Anyway, the presentations were today. Radhika's was fabulous, and Bella's was not. She ended it by showing photos and video of private moments between me and Radhika. She tried to blackmail us into giving her the position."

Kari held up a hand. "Wait. She was spying on you?"

"Yeah. She said that Radhika was only sleeping with me to get a promotion. I told Dean I quit so I wouldn't have to deal with her bullshit anymore. I can always get a new job."

Kari shook her head. "I'm confused. You're out of a job now? Not her?"

Colm let out a breath. "She is, but that's the least of it. After I quit, I left the meeting room we were in so I could talk to Radhika. My last girlfriend may have robbed me blind while we were together, but Radhika's nothing like her. Radhika would *not* sleep with me to get something she wanted."

Kari pointed at him. "First, I agree with you. When I met Radhika, she was very straightforward. Second, what the hell do you mean your last girlfriend robbed you blind?"

He winced at her screech. "Keep it down. We don't need Nya running in here."

Kari got the same look on her face that their mother did when she was about to let loose for some infraction. He held up his hands to ward it off. "All right, all right. I got robbed because my last girlfriend used my name to take out several loans before she split. I filed an identity theft complaint and my lawyer worked with the bank to have them lift the lien on my place."

"There was a lien on your place?"

"She was good."

Kari narrowed her eyes at him. "Is that why you decided to move to DC?"

He lifted a shoulder. "It was part of it."

"And now you've got a relationship building with Radhika?"

"Maybe. Probably not."

"Why?"

"She ran out on me today. I was in my office packing up, and Dean came in. I was telling him that Radhika and I were together and was about to say I wasn't going to let her bitch of a boss blackmail me when we realized Radhika was standing behind him. She left, but I caught up with her in the lobby. She wouldn't let me explain and I had to let her go. I've sent her some texts trying to see if she was okay, but she hasn't responded."

Kari came over and hugged him. "I'm sorry, Colm."

He hugged her back. "Nothing for you to be sorry over. This is something we need to talk about. She'll come around."

"I hope so for your sake. I like having happy Colm around, not grumpy Colm."

He smiled and gave her another quick hug. "I'll see where Marcus is at with the burgers."

"Good. I'll get Nya ready."

They enjoyed a nice family meal, making plans to see a baseball game and a soccer game the coming weekend.

Colm was sitting out under the stars later watching the fire in the fire pit. A small hand patted his arm. He looked down to see a nightgown-clothed Nya holding out a plastic bag to him. "Mores, please, Unca Comb."

He smiled and lifted her onto his lap. He gave her a quick kiss on the top of her head. "I'm afraid I don't have any crackers and chocolate, sweet baby."

"Okay." She dug her hand into the bag, grabbing a couple of the marshmallows and threw them into the fire.

"No." He stood up with her in his arms and retreated into the house. "No throwing the marshmallows into the fire. That's not nice."

Her lower lip started trembling as he walked into the house. "Kari, I think your daughter's ready for bed."

Kari turned around. "What? Nya! What are you doing out of bed?"

"Wanted mores. Unca Comb yelled."

With her hands on her hips, Kari walked over to them. "I'm sure he had good reason to, little miss." She reached up and took Nya out of his arms. "Thanks. I'll put her back to bed." Kari wrestled the marshmallows out of Nya's grip and passed them to Colm.

Once Kari headed upstairs, Colm went to the pantry and grabbed the graham crackers and chocolate. He didn't know where Marcus had stashed the s'mores skewers, so he pulled a fork out of the drawer. Outside, he poked a marshmallow onto the fork and roasted it up.

As he watched it turn from a bright white to golden brown, he let his thoughts turn to the last time he did this. His first kiss with Radhika after that weekend together. He should have known then he was sunk. He hadn't been ready to admit to anything other than a fling, but every time they were together, she dug a little deeper under his skin.

He thought they'd gone beyond the point of her rejecting him the way she did this afternoon. Hell, this time last night, they were burning up the sheets in his apartment. The marshmallow flared up. He removed it from the flames and blew it out.

Colm thought about going back to his apartment, but without Radhika there, he didn't want to. The memories were too fresh.

He ate the s'more and wanted nothing more than to share it with her. His phone vibrated in his pocket. Pulling it out, he hastily swallowed the sweet confection. "Radhika. Are you okay?"

Her voice was soft when she finally responded. "Maybe. Can we talk?"

"Sure. I'm at Kari and Marcus's, but they're inside."

"I'm sorry for running out on you."

He closed his eyes. "I don't understand why you didn't give me a chance to explain what was happening."

"Fear."

"What are you afraid of?"

"You."

Shocked, he dropped what was left of the s'more in the grass. "What?"

Her short laugh was strained. "I'm afraid of what will happen to my heart with you. You telling Dean about us after I had explicitly asked you not to say anything felt like I was right not to trust you."

Colm began to rub his closed eyes, but felt the melted sugar stick to his eyebrow. "Ouch."

"I'm so sorry, Colm."

"What? Oh. Not you. At least, not entirely. I had good reason to tell him. Bella was trying to blackmail me with those photos and videos I told you about. She hired someone to take pictures of us together."

"What?!"

"Yeah. There was a guy outside the restaurant last night and he followed us back to my apartment. There's a picture of us kissing." He didn't want to tell her about her office being bugged. "After you left, I went back upstairs to get the rest of my stuff. The head of HR was waiting for me. Bella was being escorted out of the building as her termination was effective immediately. As far as they're concerned, my disclosure of our prior relationship was enough notice to satisfy the company policy. They just need you to stop in to file your own disclosure the next time you're in the office."

"But everyone knows?"

He heard the anxiety in her voice and softened his to try to comfort her. "Only the people who absolutely need to know. If she tries to do anything with those photos and videos, we can sue her for invasion of privacy. The brass will let it get out that she was fired for attempted blackmail in relation to using them."

Radhika's sigh echoed in his ear. "You're at your sister's?"

"Yes."

"Can I meet you at your place?"

He closed his eyes and gave a quick mental thanks. "I can be there in five minutes."

"I'm at Hilda's in Alexandria, so it'll take me a little longer."

"I'll let the security guard know to send you up."

"Colm?"

"Yes?"

"Thank you for not telling me to go jump in the Bay."

He smiled. "Thank you for reaching out to talk with me."

20

$\mathcal{T}$hirty minutes later, Radhika was in the elevator on her way up to Colm's. The doors opened, and she walked down the hallway to his apartment. After raising her hand to knock, she paused. Was she ready to have this out with him?

Yes.

She'd been enough of a coward today as it was. She knocked. A minute later, Colm opened the door. She had a brief sense of déjà vu as she had walked through this doorway twenty-four hours ago. Then, she'd been anticipating hot sex with Colm. Now? Now she had no idea what to expect.

He led the way into the living room. "Can I get you something to drink?"

She licked her lips and saw his eyes flare as he caught the motion. An answering burn began low in her belly. "No. I'm good."

"Have a seat."

Radhika placed her purse on the table and sat down on the love seat. She wasn't sure what to do with her hands, so she stuffed them underneath her thighs. Once he sat down on the couch closest to her, she let the words spill out. "I'm sorry. I shouldn't have run out on you. I'm sorry I didn't give you a chance to explain."

His lips tightened, but he reached out and rested his hand on her knee and squeezed. "Why?"

She bit her lip and looked at the ceiling. No. No more hiding. She looked back at him. "Like I said earlier: fear." She took a deep breath and forced herself to continue. "I was hurt after Vince. I hid away. Working for Bella didn't help as I got too focused on surviving her. I never really dealt with what happened to me with Vince because of that.

"When you came, I thought I could keep things light. Last night, after we were together, I knew that wasn't possible."

"Radhika."

She shook her head. "Please. Let me finish."

"Okay."

"When I came to your office earlier and heard you tell Dean we were together, I felt like I had the rug ripped out from under me. I panicked. Stacey and Jorie kidnapped me for dinner at Hilda's. They pointed out to me that I wasn't exactly acting like an adult. I know I have trust issues, and I want to work through them. I'll go back to my therapist, whatever you decide. But, I hope you'll take me back."

She waited for him to respond, but all he did was tug on her arm. When he tugged again, she got a clue and let him pull her into his lap. He cupped her face and kissed her. The tangy mix of sweetness and heat burned through her and she shifted, brushing up against his hardening erection.

He groaned and broke the kiss. "Ah, Radhika. Yes. I wasn't looking for anything beyond a fling with someone I liked, either. You make me want to grow those roots we talked about." He rubbed his thumb against her lower lip. "We've got time, and working together on the project is going to be intense. You may want to kill me at the end of it."

She smiled and nipped the pad of his thumb. "I promise to talk out any issues with you. I won't run again."

"Good." He kissed her again. They fell back onto the couch, their limbs in a tangle. When Colm ran his hand up under her shirt, she moaned. He broke away for a moment. "Let's move this into the bedroom."

"Uh-huh." She kicked off her flats. He shifted out from under her and pulled her up. She released his hand to strip off her jacket and top.

Colm growled and put his arms around her hips, lifting her until she wrapped her legs around his waist. She bent her head and kissed him. Their tongues dueled as he walked them down the hall. He stopped and leaned back. "Bed."

"Yes."

He lowered her down onto it and trailed kisses along her collarbone. She dug her fingers into his hair and lifted her chest up so he could undo her bra. He pulled it off her arms and moved from her shoulders to her breasts.

The pull of suction on her nipple had her legs shifting as her body readied itself for him. His hands dug under the waistband of her leggings. Colm kneeled up and stripped them off along with her panties. His eyes darkened. "You are gorgeous."

"Enough for the Hurricane Hottie?"

Colm bent down, stopping when his lips were millimeters from hers. "The Hurricane Hottie is no more. He belongs only to you."

She smiled poured all the feelings she had for him into the kiss. "You. Naked. Now."

He complied and returned to worship her body. After his attentions sent her over the first peak of the night, she did some worshipping of her own. She drew in a deep breath of his scent while kissing his chest. "I never want to let you go."

Colm must have heard her as he hugged her. "I'm never letting you go either. You can run, but I'll find you. Together, Radhika."

She pushed him onto his back and sheathed his erection, first with the condom he'd pulled from his nightstand and then with her own body. Looking into his eyes, she repeated the promise as she rode him to completion. "Together, Colm."

AWARDS SEASON

Colm led a tired and slightly drunk Radhika into the suite he'd rented for their stay in Los Angeles. It sucked to have lost the award, but they'd been nominated. He always played to win, but Radhika was a huge reason why they'd been nominated and he was so proud of her.

Any lingering talk from her time with Vince was history. Colm didn't care if he was petty, but watching Vince's very public firing from the morning news show—for inappropriate relations with a staff member—from where he'd been waiting in the wings to go on for his guest appearance had been sweet.

Radhika danced to some song only she heard as she went to the kitchenette area and pulled out the bottle of champagne he'd placed there earlier. She pointed at him. "If anyone tells you it was just an honor to be nominated, don't believe them. I wanted that award."

He nodded. "I know you did, honey."

"We should have won."

"They had a hookier and sexier concept. We made people care about climate change legislation." In fact, their series had created a national conversation around a set of air quality regulations that were due to expire, and they'd heard from Anita's contacts on the Hill that there had been a spike of calls to legislators about them. If he had to choose only one reward for his work, he'd go with public engagement on a topic he was passionate about.

Speaking of topics he was passionate about, the other one was motioning to him with a bottle opener.

"I can't get this."

He walked over to her and took the opener out of her hand, smacking a kiss on her lips. "You are gorgeous tonight."

Radhika's grin lit up the room, and she wrapped her arms around his neck. "You are the sweetest man in the world." She paused. "I am also a bit drunk."

"I noticed."

She regally inclined her head and waved her hand to the bottle. "Then get to work on helping me keep this buzz going."

He set the opener on the counter and reached into his pocket for the box he'd placed there as they'd gotten ready for the awards show earlier. He hadn't been planning on doing anything as gauche as giving it to her on stage if they'd won. For one thing, he knew she'd tell him no and walk off the stage, middle fingers flying high.

Colm popped the top of the box, hoping she'd like the platinum-set cluster of diamonds. "Radhika, you showed me that while I was looking to the sky, I had the ability to grow roots and make my life with someone who could ground me."

Her hands were covering her mouth and tears ran down her cheeks.

"I love you. Will you please marry me?"

She closed her eyes and nodded. "You've had it with you all night?"

"Yeah. I knew even if we won that there was a greater award waiting for me if you said yes."

Her laugh was watery, but she kissed him. "Yes. I love you, too. You're definitely better than some gold statue that I'd only have to polish."

Colm grinned. "Next year. I promise."

She smacked a kiss on his lips and grinned back. "Together."

"Together."

~

Loved Radhika and Colm's story? Please leave a review!

Stacey is up next in THE BRIDESMAID AND THE SPY, with an expected release of Fall/Winter 2017/18.

Sign up for Kelly's newsletter at www.kellymaher.com/contact and get notified when it releases!

ACKNOWLEDGMENTS

There are so many people I have to thank for their contributions in making this a much better book than the one I started with that I know I will miss mentioning someone. If I do, please know you have my thanks. Shayera, Wendy, MK, Jessica/Taylor, Soni, Shari, Carrie Ann, Zoe, Wednesday Night Writes, and Romance Divas, I greatly appreciate the advice and knowledge you all shared with me whenever I had questions. Andie, Michele, and Tara, thanks for being my inspiration for the Brunching Bridesmaids!! Brunch next Sunday, right?

ABOUT THE AUTHOR

Foiled in her attempts to pursue a career in Forensic Anthropology due to a fatal incomprehension of calculus, Kelly turned to a life of telling people where to go, AKA librarianship. She then took another page out of her idol Indiana Jones' playbook and renamed herself after the dog, writing tales of romance of varying heat levels and erotica. She currently splits her time working on new writing projects and at the day job in a federal library in Washington, DC.

Kelly can be found on Twitter at @kmmaher and on Facebook at facebook.com/KellyMaherAuthor.

For more information
www.kellymaher.com
Newsletter: www.kellymaher.com/contact

CPSIA information can be obtained
at www.ICGtesting.com
Printed in the USA
FFOW02n2142190518
46728883-48879FF